———————— ★ ————————

MURDER, MURDER EVERYWHERE

"I don't want to make things any more difficult for you than they are, Mrs. Summers," Chambrun said. "I told you earlier that I can't view this as a coincidence. Somebody is trying to turn your life into a gruesome nightmare. Who, Mrs. Summers? Who hates you? Who wants to harm you?"

She stared at him, eyes wide and frightened. "I...I don't have any friends, Mr. Chambrun. By the same token I don't have any enemies."

"I'm afraid I don't think so," Chambrun said. "Think!"

———————— ★ ————————

"Hugh Pentecost's suspense stories, set in New York's most elegant hotel, keep getting better and better."

—*Publishers Weekly*

HUGH PENTECOST
MURDER IN LUXURY

WORLDWIDE®

TORONTO · NEW YORK · LONDON · PARIS
AMSTERDAM · STOCKHOLM · HAMBURG
ATHENS · MILAN · TOKYO · SYDNEY

MURDER IN LUXURY

A Worldwide Mystery/April 1991

First published by Dodd, Mead & Company, Inc.

ISBN 0-373-26069-5

Printed in U.S.A.

PART ONE

ONE

LOOKING BACK at the many stories I've written about murder and violence at the Beaumont, New York's top luxury hotel, people might get the notion that that gracious and elegant establishment is not a place to stay in safety. Actually you would be as safe there, perhaps safer, than in your own home. Which, in an age of violence and terror, of vandalism and senseless brutality, is how safe?

The Beaumont is, you could say, a city within a city. It has its own security force, hospital facilities, bars, restaurants, meeting places, a shopping mall. It houses a branch of one of the country's largest and most prestigious banks. It has everything a small city has except schools. I could go cute, I suppose, and say that it houses a school in expert management, presided over by a master executive. He is Pierre Chambrun, the Beaumont's legendary manager. Some of us who work for him think he has some kind of magical radar system behind his bright, black eyes. It seems as if he can sense a malfunction in the Swiss-watch operation of the world over which he presides before it happens. Unfortunately he can't change human nature. He can't eliminate greed, or jealousy, or a passion for revenge, or the impulse to treachery or betrayal in the individual man or woman. And so, as in every other place on earth, these ugly psychoses disrupt men's efforts to live peaceful and orderly lives.

It was one of these dark and twisted passions that brought Valerie Summers into our world—the Beaumont. She brought with her a trail of murders that baffled even Chambrun, who is usually way ahead of the police. To me she brought something personally disturbing. Was I to fall in love with a charming and gentle girl who needed affection and understanding and care, or with a monster hiding behind a lovely face?

But, to the beginning.

The day that Valerie Summers came on stage was like any other day. Routines at the Beaumont are fixed. At eight-thirty every morning Chambrun is served an elaborate gourmet breakfast in his office on the second floor. At nine o'clock I, his public relations man, put in an appearance, along with Betsy Ruysdale, his fabulous secretary. She brings with her the registration cards of the people who have checked into the hotel since the morning before. Our guests might have been somewhat surprised had they known the information that appears on those cards. There is, not unexpectedly, a credit rating. But there are other symbols that indicated whether a man—or a woman— is an alcoholic, a man or a woman chaser, gay, lesbian, a husband double-crossing a wife or a wife double-crossing a husband. We are close to the United Nations and many of our guests are from other parts of the world. The cards reveal where they are from, their politics, their business in our city. There is sometimes a special symbol which indicates that Chambrun knows something about the guest that is not to be made available to the rest of the staff. Hundreds of people sleep under our roof each night and Chambrun knows more about them than most people know about their children.

The reason for my presence at these morning sessions is to be able to handle anything special in connection with a new guest. We may have a movie star or a foreign dignitary who wants the world to know that he is here, or he may want privacy and perhaps to remain incognito. It's my job to handle the press and the media, whichever way the wind blows.

There was nothing that morning that needed special attention and I was just about to leave when the little red light on the phone on Chambrun's desk blinked. Betsy Ruysdale answered. After listening she covered the mouthpiece with her hand.

"Gardner Fails is at the front desk," she said. "It's something of an emergency. Can he come up?"

"Of course," Chambrun said.

Gardner Fails is one of the trustees of the corporate entity that owns the Beaumont. He's a lawyer, a "man of distinction" in his late fifties. Chambrun signaled to me to wait. If Fails wanted some sort of special service I might be the agent the Man would use.

Chambrun's office is more like a gracious living room than a place of business. His desk is carved Florentine, the rug a priceless oriental, and there are books, paintings, in particular a blue-period Picasso, a gift from the great artist himself. Not long ago a film company was considering one of my stories about Chambrun. I was asked to suggest an actor who might play the role of the Great Man. Unfortunately the perfect choice is no longer available—the late Claude Rains. Chambrun is short, stocky, but elegant in his manner and movements. His dark eyes are buried in deep pouches. They can twinkle with humor, glow warm with compassion, or turn as cold as a hanging judge's. His clothes are custom tailored, his shirts, ties, and shoes made to order. He is something of a Beau Brummell, but he handles it without affectation.

I could sense a resistance stiffening in him as we waited for Gardner Fails. The trustees, as a rule, don't make sensible requests or suggestions. Chambrun, I knew, would listen with courtesy and patience, but if his answer was no, no one would override him.

Miss Ruysdale ushered in Gardner Fails. He had a mane of carefully styled gray hair and bushy, black eyebrows. I suspected that his tan came from a sunlamp and not outdoor exposure. He and Chambrun greeted each other with smiles.

"You know Mark Haskell, my public relations genius," Chambrun said.

I had met Fails several times but evidently I hadn't made an impression. He shook hands cordially with a stranger.

"Small problem, Pierre," he said, turning back to Chambrun.

"Small problems are always easier to handle than big ones," Chambrun said. He leaned back in his desk chair and lit one of his flat, Egyptian cigarettes.

"Business is apparently good," Fails said. "I went to the front desk to get a room for a client and they tell me there is nothing available."

"If they tell you that, it's so," Chambrun said.

Fails' smile widened. "It occurred to me you might know something that they don't know at the desk," he said.

If you are a theatergoer you know that most managements hold out what they call "house seats." These are seats kept in reserve for famous people, old friends who want to get into a hit show at the last minute. We've adopted the phrase at the Beaumont—house seats. A couple of single rooms, a suite, are kept available for an unexpected movie star, a political or diplomatic bigwig, or an old friend. They are not made available to anyone without Chambrun's approval. It wasn't my business to mention them. Chambrun knew about them and if they were still available. It was up to him.

"You listen to the news on television or the radio this morning?" Fails asked.

"I never listen," Chambrun said. "I count on Mark to let me know if there's a tidal wave approaching."

"I have a radio in the bathroom while I shave," I said.

"You hear an item about a lady who came home from the theater last night and found a man murdered in her apartment?"

"Down in the Village somewhere," I said.

"West Tenth Street," Fails said. "The lady, Valerie Summers, is my client."

Chambrun's eyes were narrowed against the smoke from his cigarette. He looked only mildly interested.

"A mess," Fails said. "Val had been to see that musical with Mickey Rooney and Ann Miller—what is it, *Sugar Babies*? Went by herself, which is part of the story. Came home. It's a ground-floor garden apartment in a remodeled brownstone. No sign of trouble. Let herself in with her key and found a dead man, shot through the head, soaking in his own blood in the middle of her living room rug."

"I didn't pay much attention to the story," I said. "Murders are a dime a dozen these days. I seem to remember your lady didn't know the dead man."

"Never laid eyes on him before in her life," Fails said. "Complete stranger. You can imagine, she was pretty well shaken up; called the police. They gave her a hard time until she had the opportunity to call me."

"Why?" Chambrun said.

"Why what, Pierre?"

"Why did they give her a hard time?"

"There was no sign of a break-in," Fails said. "No sign anyone had tried to rob the apartment. Homicide cop who was called in just didn't believe Val. Cops have sort of black-and-white categories when they look at a crime. Apparently not a robbery, no forced entry, no evidence of a missing person who might have been the killer. So this Homicide man, a Lieutenant Keegan, fitted it into the slot that reads 'lovers' quarrel.' He chose not to believe Val when she said she'd never seen the dead man before, anywhere."

"Dead man identified?" Chambrun asked.

"Not as of now," Fails said. "No wallet, no papers, no keys, no credit cards. They're checking out fingerprints."

"Your Miss Summers must have friends who would know if the dead man was someone she knew or saw," Chambrun said.

"It's 'Mrs.' Summers," Fails said. "Her story didn't help convince Keegan. You see, she doesn't have friends who are that close to her. You have time for me to fill you in a little, Pierre?"

"I'll take time," Chambrun said.

"Val is thirty years old," Fails said. "Beautiful girl—woman. She is—was—the daughter of Jeb McCandless. You remember him, Pierre?"

"I never knew him," Chambrun said, "but I remember who he was. Oil, steel, anything that turns to gold."

Fails nodded. "Married several times. No children until the last time when he married a girl forty years his junior. She died in childbirth, bringing Valerie into the world. Valerie became the center of his late years. Brought up with nurses, tutors, finally a fine education—Vassar. It's a girls' college, or was. Nowadays they mix the sexes everywhere. Val met a young man there, Richard Summers, fell in love with him, married him after graduation."

"Over Papa McCandless's dead body?"

"No. Jeb liked Dick Summers. I was Jeb's lawyer, you know. My father before me. I know he was pleased. Dick went on to law school and Jeb helped keep the young couple afloat till Dick was ready to take on his responsibilities as a husband. He came from a small town in Ohio; he and Val went to live there, where he set up in private law practice. He was a winner, that boy. He bought a small house and they settled in there, forever I guess they thought. Jeb died about five years ago and left Val one of the richest young women in America. That didn't change her and Dick's life style. I think she saw the money as a means of doing good things for other people—cancer research, that sort of thing, supporting the arts, theater, music, dance. They lived, basically, on what Dick earned, and he was doing damned well."

"You keep saying 'was,'" Chambrun said.

"Unfortunately. About eight months ago Dick went to the county seat to defend a client in a lawsuit. He stayed in a hotel there. He talked to Val on the phone the first night he was there. She hadn't gone with him because she was involved in some kind of community project. There was a fire in that hotel later that night—and Dick didn't make it. They brought him home—a charred, unrecognizable corpse."

"Rough," I heard myself say.

"It was more than Val could take," Fails said. "They had been so much, so perfectly, in love. She couldn't bear to stay in the house where they'd lived together, she couldn't stand the sympathy of friends who had been *their* friends. All she wanted to do was get away from the place that was haunted by Dick's ghost."

"She could afford to go anywhere," Chambrun said.

"Yes. She called me. She thought New York would be an ideal place. She could be anonymous here; nobody would know who she was; there'd be no small-town neighbors who knew her story. She needed time to be alone—'to beat the heat,' she told me. So, I found her the apartment on Tenth Street and she came East. I urged her to make friends, offered to introduce her to young people I knew. She wanted none of that—not yet. So, I kept in touch with her from time to time. It seemed wrong to me for her to be so alone, but in the end, I thought, time would take care of it. Then last night she called me. There had been a murder, and there was a suspicious cop who had read her her rights and given her her legal phone call.''

Chambrun put out his cigarette in the brass ashtray on his desk. "You say her story didn't convince this Lieutenant Keegan. Why not?"

The lawyer's face turned hard. "Because he's determined to make everything fit his 'lovers' quarrel' category," Fails said. "He read me his scenario when I got there. Young beautiful widow living alone in the big city, no friends, no regular man in her life. Probably sex starved, he said to me. The Village is full of bars and clubs where a lonely woman might go. She picks up a likely looking man, brings him home. Something goes wrong and she shoots him dead."

"Weapon?" Chambrun asked. "A gun?"

"If there had been Val would be under arrest," Fails said. "Cops are combing the Village for places where she might have gone and been recognized, where the dead man might have been known. Meanwhile she can't stay in the apartment, cops in and out. It will take a massive cleanup job to make the place livable again. I brought her to my office, which you know is just a couple of blocks from here. I thought the Beaumont would be a sanctuary for her."

Chambrun, I saw, had made up his mind. "It happens there is a small suite available on the fifth floor," he said. "Living room, couple of bedrooms, couple of baths, kitchenette. It's expensive."

"If money was the answer she could rent five suites," Fails said. "She needs friends without asking for them, help without asking for it. Here, I thought, there would be you, Miss Ruysdale if she needed a woman's understanding, Haskell here if she needed someone in her own age bracket who might buy her a drink, or a dinner, or help her to laugh a little—if that's possible.''

Chambrun leaned back in his chair. "I guess you've sold me, Gardner," he said. "We'll be glad to welcome your Mrs. Summers.''

TWO

SOMETIMES, when it comes to women, I am not an entirely admirable character. I am reminded of a remark by the late George Kauffman, witty playwright, about someone he didn't like too much. "Down deep I think he's rather shallow."

Glamorous women are very much a part of our world at the Beaumont—movie stars, famous actresses, the cream of the crop in the social swim, mysterious beauties from the far ends of the earth. My job brings me into closer touch with them all than any other member of the staff. The result, I have said somewhere else, is that I tend to fall in love forever every few months. That may not suggest a very solid person, but I have to say that it's provided me with more sheer pleasure than I would care to have missed for the sake of a more rock-ribbed image.

I was assigned by Chambrun to be ready for the arrival of Valerie Summers. I waited at the front desk for Gardner Fails to produce his client. Beautiful, rich, lovely, and in trouble; those ingredients don't add up to the worst prospect in the world.

The word *beautiful* gets overused when it's applied to women. There are millions of them with handsomely boned faces and elegant, lush figures. Real beauty comes from some kind of inner electricity, some special supply of energy. Without that internal magic they don't light up, are no more interesting than an expertly painted clothes dummy in a store window. Conversely, women who do have it but lack the classic mold and measurements can still take center stage. As if you didn't know if you have an eye for women!

I have seen Hollywood glamor queens sweep into the lobby at the Beaumont, surrounded by bellboys with luggage, gentlemen with dreams, other women with a tight-lipped look of envy on their faces. It can be a production, with all eyes turned their way.

Valerie Summers' arrival was a nothing. She walked in from the street with her lawyer, he carrying a small, insignificant suitcase. The lady was something of a disappointment. She was wearing a plain, navy-blue summer dress, trimmed with a little white stuff at the neck and the cuffs of the long sleeves. Figure? Good, but you wouldn't turn to look again or whistle at her from the front of the corner drugstore. Her hair was gold, worn shoulder length—her most notable feature. I couldn't tell much about her face because she was wearing large, dark-tinted sunglasses. Her mouth was set in a firm, straight line, like someone about to walk with courage into the lion's den. Wounded, I thought. When you can't see a woman's eyes you can't tell what's cooking.

Fails introduced us. "Mrs. Summers, Mark Haskell."

"Hello," she said. It was a low, almost husky voice. Scared out of her wits, I thought. Well, you don't stumble on a dead man in your apartment, lying in a pool of blood, and find a tough Homicide cop suspecting you of murder, and laugh your way out of it.

"My pleasure to take you up to your suite, Mrs. Summers," I said. I beckoned to a waiting bellboy to take the lone suitcase. "Mr. Chambrun has already registered you so we can go straight up."

"I'm going to leave you to Mark, my dear," Fails said. "I'm already very late for a business appointment. If there's any problem don't hesitate to call. I'll arrange for you to be put straight through."

I found myself jabbering like an idiot as I walked Valerie across the lobby toward the south bank of elevators. Like a tour guide, I thought afterward, pointing to the shops, the bars and restaurants, the entrance to the Blue Lagoon, the popular nightclub that isn't, of course, open in the late morning.

That firm, almost forbidding mouth of Valerie's relaxed in the tiniest of little smiles. "You're not obliged to try to entertain me, Mr. Haskell," she said.

"It's not an obligation, Mrs. Summers. It would be a pleasure if I had a clue to what would amuse you."

She and I and the bellboy were on the self-service elevator. The boy pushed the right button. The doors closed, noiselessly. The car started up—noiselessly. I glanced at Valerie and at the same moment she glanced at me. Both our heads were tilted back, looking up; not that we could see where we were going. I smiled at her.

"Symbolic," I said. "Off into the wild blue yonder."

She looked away. It hadn't struck her as so damned witty. I realized that after what she'd been through in the last hours even Groucho Marx goosing Margaret Dumont wouldn't produce a laugh. I remembered the haughty Miss Dumont saying to Groucho, "Do I

make myself plain?'' and Groucho replying, ''Well,
certainly somebody did.'' The quiet girl standing next
to me had to be thinking about a man lying in his own
blood with a hole in his head. Not a laughing matter.

We got off at the fifth floor and the bellboy let us
into Five A, the suite Chambrun had pulled out of his
hat for Valerie. No two suites in the Beaumont are
decorated exactly alike. Five A was better suited for a
British diplomat than a young American woman.
There were a couple of paintings of scarlet-coated
riders following a pack of hounds; there was a sea-
scape of waves breaking against a rugged coastline
somewhere; the furnishings were elegant Victorian.

On the center table in the living room was a bou-
quet of spring flowers, a small envelope propped
against the vase. Valerie made no move toward the
envelope.

''Mr. Fails?'' she asked.

''Fresh flowers and a bottle of champagne in your
kitchen cooler are standard welcomes from the Beaumont's management,'' I said.

''How very nice,'' she said, without enthusiasm.

The bellboy returned from leaving her bag in one of
the bedrooms down the corridor. He stood there in the
doorway. It was tip time but she didn't seem to notice. I signaled to him to take off. I'd handle it later.

The sound of the outer door closing as the boy left
seemed to bring Valerie back into the world. She
turned to me, reached up, and took off those dark
glasses. I actually felt my legs go wobbly. She had the
most extraordinary, violet-colored eyes I've ever seen.
The word *beautiful* suddenly fitted her, with all it's
supposed to mean.

"Don't ever put on those glasses again," I said.

"I don't understand."

"With those eyes?"

She turned away. I didn't seem to know how to play it right with her. Then she turned back and those eyes were deep, tragic wells. I wanted to reach out to her, to protect her.

"Is it Mark ... your first name?" she asked.

I said it was.

"You've tried so hard to be cheerful and friendly, and I ... I'm such a clod!" she said.

"I've just been trying to find the right tune to play," I said.

"Mr. Fails has told you why I'm here?"

"Yes. There's nothing much one can say to make that experience less shocking."

"That's all he told you? About last night, and the police, and all that?"

"He told us why you are living in New York," I said.

"'Us'?"

"Mr. Chambrun and me."

"Chambrun. I hear he's some kind of a god who runs the hotel."

"Some kind of a god ... and a very decent, compassionate man."

She turned to the flowers again, her back to me. I thought I saw a little shudder move along her shoulders. "I don't seem to be able to learn how to function alone," she said. "My husband and I ... well, we were two parts of one person. With him I could have faced the ghastly business last night without turning a hair. Alone ..." She shook her golden head from side to side. "Do you know that policeman thinks I'm some kind of a whore out looking for sex in the local saloons?"

"Fails mentioned it," I said. "Policemen tend to try to make each new crime fit a standard pattern. When that one doesn't prove out for your man he'll try to fit it into some other familiar category. Then he'll go away and let you be."

She looked around the room. She sounded a little desperate when she spoke. "I had to change myself around, find some new approach to living each day, after Dick was killed. The apartment downtown is my place, my things, a little piece of my world. This—" and she gestured around "—this isn't mine. It's strange. It's just not mine."

"People with troubles like yours—and I'm talking about your husband, not this other mess—often travel, go to different and new places, try a cruise, perhaps. They don't have friends when they start, but they make them along the way. Maybe not forever, but just to pass the time." I smiled at her. "Well, here I am, a presentable young man—thirty-eight years young. There's Chambrun, a charming gent if you want to talk about the arts, or music, or the fascinating guests at the Beaumont. There's Betsy Ruysdale, his secretary, an exceptional gal if you want someone for woman-talk. We're all ready if you'll give us a chance."

"I'm very grateful, but..."

"I can show you the sights, take you dining and dancing if you like. There's an art show in the gallery. I can take you for a drive in the park in a horse-drawn cab." I waved at the television set in the corner. "Of course, if you prefer Archie Bunker..."

"You're very sweet, Mark," she said. "I'm afraid, for a little while, I'm going to just have to slug it out alone."

"I can't twist your arm," I said. "If you need anything at all, call my office. If you need something serious, call Chambrun. If you want to cry on someone's shoulder, call Betsy Ruysdale. I'll be back later in the day—just in case."

So I left her, regretting I hadn't been able to ring the right bell.

THERE ARE BASES for me to cover every day at the Beaumont. There are fashion shows where glamorous models display the latest from Paris or Seventh Avenue to buyers for the "Beautiful People"; there are small conventions, and directors' meetings for big corporations, Hollywood stars, best-selling authors, sports figures, and special friends of someone who need an individual and cordial hello. My job is to greet, to find out if they want the press brought in or kept out, and to let them know that the whole staff is in the starting blocks, prepared to make it clear that they are now in the best of all possible worlds. It would be a bore if the faces weren't different every day.

I left Valerie Summers to go through these standard routines, but I wasn't quite able to shake the tragedy in those wide violet eyes, an air of helpless desperation. What she needed, I thought, was to be taken out of an atmosphere that bore any relationship to her regular life. Absurdly, I thought of a rollercoaster ride at Coney Island and sticks of cotton candy—and the tunnel of love?

A little before noon I checked into Chambrun's office. Ruysdale was at her desk in the outer room. Chambrun never calls her Betsy or Miss Ruysdale. He neuters her by simply calling her Ruysdale. The whisper persists among the staff that their relationship is a lot closer than that impersonal "Ruysdale" suggests. She's a handsome woman with natural red hair and the milk-white skin that often goes with that coloring. She dresses rather severely in the office. Chambrun wouldn't have liked having an army of males hanging around his chief aide. I've seen her, however, at a charity ball, wearing a low-cut evening gown. She is something! I remember wondering why I was wasting my time with young women. Ruysdale is, I suppose, about forty, but very much in her prime.

She gestured toward Chambrun's office. "The long arm of the law," she said.

"What have we done now?"

"We are clean," Ruysdale said. "It's Lieutenant Matthew Keegan, the Homicide man in charge of the Summers case. You get the lady settled in?"

"*Settled* isn't the word I'd choose. Shook-up lady."

"I think the Man would appreciate an interruption," Ruysdale said. "Why don't you just walk in?"

Having heard Gardner Fails suggest that Keegan was probably an old-fashioned kind of cop trying to make a crime fit a familiar pattern—and having assured Valerie Summers that that's the way it was—the Homicide man was unexpected. "Matthew Keegan" suggested a face like the map of Ireland and square-toed shoes. The man sitting in a leather armchair fac-

ing Chambrun across the carved, Florentine desk
looked like a bright young Madison Avenue advertis-
ing genius; well-tailored tropical worsted summer suit,
pale gray, what I would have sworn were custom-made
shoes, well polished, a pale blue Brooks Brothers shirt
with a button-down collar, and a dark-blue silk tie
with maroon stripes. This young detective was a fashion plate. He had dark curly hair, worn short, and
dark eyes that had a twinkle of humor in them. I've
called him young, but I suppose he was my age, late
thirties. It depends on how old you are how young that
is. I was to learn later that Keegan was college edu-
cated with a law degree from Columbia. He belonged
to what Chambrun called "a new breed of cop." This
one hadn't learned his crime-fighting techniques by
first pounding a beat.

Chambrun introduced us and I had the uncomfortable feeling for a moment that those keen dark eyes
were reading the label on the inside of my shirt collar.
This, I thought, could be a weakness. Keegan had
formed an opinion about me before I had opened my
mouth to say boo.

"Mark has been settling in Mrs. Summers,"
Chambrun said.

"Couple of hours ago," I said.

"How does she seem?" Chambrun asked.

"What would you expect? Dead strangers on your
living room rug are not a cause for celebration," I
said.

"Particularly if you gunned them down yourself,"
Keegan said. It was a thin, steely voice that, I found
out after a while, made everything he said sound
threatening.

"The Lieutenant has a little more information than we had from Gardner Fails," Chambrun said. He was leaning back in his desk chair, heavy eyelids lowered, with a faint smile on his lips. I knew that Cheshire-cat look. He was pleased with himself about something.

"We have identified the dead man," Keegan said. "He used several names in his business, but we think the real one was Carl Rogers. He was known in the Village. A peddler."

"Drugs?" I asked.

"Drugs, porno-sex, anything lousy you can think of," Keegan said. "He's been charged more than a dozen times with crimes of one sort or another, but he's always managed to slip off the hook. There are two possible angles to his case."

"It's a little early to limit yourself to two, isn't it, Lieutenant?" Chambrun suggested.

Keegan gave Chambrun what I thought was a mildly patronizing smile. "I don't think we'll have to go beyond two," he said. "Studying people is my business, you know."

"If you'll stop to think about it, so is mine," Chambrun said.

"You don't know Mrs. Summers, do you?"

"I haven't laid eyes on her yet," Chambrun said.

"I was called in on the case about one o'clock this morning," Keegan said. "Her story was she'd been to a show—musical with Mickey Rooney—and got home a little after eleven o'clock. Let herself into her apartment, she says, switched on the lights, and there was a man, shot in the head, just lying there. She called the local precinct house. A couple of patrol cops got there first, then two detectives from the precinct. When they were satisfied it was a homicide I was called in. My department.''

"What convinced the original detectives it was a homicide?" I asked. Foolish question, I suppose.

"No guns anywhere," Keegan said. "Somebody shot Carl Rogers and took off, or—" and Keegan's eyes narrowed "—somebody shot Rogers, disposed of the gun, and didn't take off."

"Meaning Mrs. Summers?" Chambrun said.

"Who else?"

"You haven't found the gun?"

"Not yet. The medical examiner got the body about midnight. He guesses Rogers had been dead three to four hours. That would place the shooting at some time between eight and nine o'clock."

"Mrs. Summers was at the theater then," Chambrun said.

"She says. She has no ticket stub to prove it. She was alone, she says. No one to alibi her. There is absolutely no sign of any forced entry to the apartment. Back door locked, no windows forced, not even a scratch on the front-door lock."

"Rogers was a professional criminal," Chambrun said. "He could have managed a simple lock, couldn't he?"

"He'd have had to have something to do it with," Keegan said. "A skeleton key, a lock pick of some kind. Nothing like that on the body."

"I understand from Gardner Fails he had no wallet, no identification of any kind," Chambrun said.

"True. Just a few bucks in bills and loose change. We identified him from the fingerprint files. They had his prints from one of those early arrests."

"And you think . . ."

"Mrs. Summers had to have let Rogers into the apartment," Keegan said.

"Isn't there someone else who had access? A building superintendent, a janitor?"

"Man who covers several buildings on the block. He was home all evening playing poker with friends. Airtight alibi. He has a key, but it never left him. The building owner may have a key. He's in Europe."

"Some previous tenant?"

"Woman who had the apartment before Mrs. Summers died about a year ago. She was ninety-two years old. No family. No maid who came in and might have had a key. Mrs. Summers has no cleaning woman or a maid with a key. Can you imagine a woman with her kind of money having no help?"

Chambrun reached in the cedar-lined box on his desk for a cigarette. "So you have two theories, Lieutenant."

"There's something abnormal about a young, beautiful, very rich chick being so alone," Keegan said.

"You know her story," Chambrun said. "A happy marriage, her husband burned up in a fire. It takes time for someone to adjust after a thing like that."

"It's how they adjust," Keegan said. "Drugs are a way to adjust. Some kind of raw sex is a way to adjust. Carl Rogers was in the business of supplying both those things."

"So?"

"So she went hunting for one or both," Keegan said. "When it began I can't guess just yet. Rogers could have been supplying the lady with whatever she needed for months. Then, he either held her up, cut off her supply, tried to blackmail her and she let him have it."

"Blackmail?"

"Hell, Mr. Chambrun, the Village is like a small town. Word about people gets around. To begin with, Gardner Fails found that apartment for her. I guess he made no secret to the renting agent who his client was. Jeb McCandless's daughter, a very, very rich lady. Rogers would hear that sooner or later. He put the bite on her for some really big dough. Maybe he threatened to expose her habits, whatever they are."

"So she kills her source of supply?"

"Maybe not. Maybe I've got her wrong," Keegan said. "My number two theory is that Rogers didn't know her, but heard about her, knew who she was, that she was loaded. He studied her, rang her doorbell last night, threatened her, God knows what, and she shot him."

"And then goes calmly to the theater and doesn't report it for three or four hours?"

"She had to get rid of the gun," Keegan said. "I doubt if she went to the theater."

"It would be strange, if she did go to the theater," I said, "that there isn't someone who will remember that head of beautiful golden blonde hair."

"So what?" Keegan said. "Maybe she did go. She had to have time to think her way out of the jam she was in."

"What kind of a jam was she in?" Chambrun asked. He sounded suddenly impatient. "A common crook, drug pusher, con man, gets himself admitted to her apartment with some tall story and threatens her. She acts in self-defense.''

"And waits three or four hours to call the police? That's what's wrong with my number two theory, Mr. Chambrun. If Rogers was a complete stranger and threatened her, why wait to report it? No, I have to think they had some kind of relationship. He supplied her with drugs; maybe he, personally, supplied her with sex, or with young studs to do the job; or with a gay woman if she's that kind. They quarreled over money, over who knows what. She shoots him. Then she needed time to get calmed down. Maybe there's blood on her clothes. She has to change and get rid of bloody clothes *and* the gun before she calls the police.''

"And you haven't a shred of evidence to prove any of that, Lieutenant, or she wouldn't be staying here at the Beaumont, free to come and go as she pleases.''

"I'll find the evidence," Keegan said. "But I don't want her taking a powder on me while I collect it.''

Chambrun glanced at me. "The lieutenant came here to ask me to put a tap on Mrs. Summers' phone," he said. "I've told him I'll do no such thing. A guest in this hotel is entitled to exactly the same security as a man in his own home. This *is* his home when he's staying here.''

"I can get a court order," Keegan said.

"Maybe," Chambrun said. "If you can and do, I won't obey it, nor will any other employee of this hotel. You'll have to close up the place and send hundreds of us to jail, Lieutenant. Get a warrant for her arrest and take her out of here and no one will resist you. Try to invade her privacy while she's a guest here and you'll find yourself behind a very large eight ball."

For a moment the two men stared at each other, adversaries. I think Keegan decided that pressure was not the way to deal with Chambrun.

"I don't understand what you'd expect to hear on her phone, Lieutenant," I said. "It isn't a private line. It goes through a switchboard. She knows that."

Keegan seemed to be thinking out loud, not answering me.

"Very rich people can afford eccentricities that the rest of us can't," he said. "Valerie McCandless Summers can afford a drug habit without any problems. She can buy herself sex partners without any problems. She can be in touch with a travel agent right now making plans to take off for China, if she thinks she'll be safe there."

"And following that line of reasoning," Chambrun said, "She could have bought off a cheap punk like Carl Rogers without any difficulty at all. She could afford to pay blackmail if that's what his game was."

"Maybe she was on a high, blew her stack," Keegan said.

"And maybe it was exactly the way she says it was," Chambrun said. "She went to the theater alone, came home, and found a dead stranger on her rug." He pushed back his chair and stood up. "I'm sorry, Lieutenant, I can't set traps for guests of the hotel to make your job easier."

A kind of dark anger flooded the detective's face. Black Irishman, I thought.

"I hope you won't come to regret making that decision, Mr. Chambrun," he said.

THREE

I SUPPOSE YOU COULD SAY that I live in a kind of fantasy world, a kid's dream-up. Nothing can go wrong with Papa in charge. Papa stands guard against all dragons, and even more than that, against all human villains who can *really* make trouble. It was a busy day, and I didn't worry about Valerie Summers, didn't even think about her till along about six o'clock—drink time. Chambrun—who is the Papa in my world—had decided to protect her against the villain, who was Lieutenant Matt Keegan of Homicide. That may sound childish, but you may have heard the television commercial for some insurance company—"Get yourself a piece of the rock." Some wise guy said, "We don't need a piece of the rock. At the Beaumont we have the rock itself." He meant Chambrun, of course. That's how we all feel.

So Valerie Summers was safe, I thought, but at six o'clock I decided she might be interested in a drink, even dinner. Gardner Fails had suggested that could be my function and the notion didn't depress me. I'm a kind of a sly operator, you should know. I called room service to ask if the lady in Five A had ordered drinks or dinner. Nothing had been served up there all day. There were a hundred places in the hotel and within a couple of blocks of it where she could have gone for lunch, of course.

I decided if I wanted her to join me I wouldn't call her on the phone. It would be too easy for her to say no. I stopped at the florist in the lobby, bought a single gardenia, went up to Five A and rang the doorbell.

Valerie opened the door after a moment. I handed her the gardenia. "You did say six-fifteen," I said.

"Six-fifteen?"

"For drinks and dinner," I said.

She glanced at the flower and managed a tentative smile. "Oh, Mark, how very nice. But I don't think..."

"You're not supposed to think. Just powder your nose—whatever that means—and we'll hit some high spots." I glanced at one of the hunting prints on the wall. "You can't sit here forever watching that same horseman taking that same hedge. At least let me buy you a drink. If after a drink you have no appetite or you find me too dull, I'll bring you back."

"Oh, Mark, I don't think...I'm the one who'll be dull."

"Your policeman friend, Keegan, poured out his heart to Chambrun and me. Wouldn't you like to know what a suspicious and dangerous character you are?"

"He's been here?"

"Been and gone, at least for now," I said.

"What does he..."

"Over a drink," I said.

It wasn't entirely flattering to me, because I think it was curiosity about Keegan that won the day. She beckoned me in, excused herself and reappeared in a very few minutes. She couldn't have had an extensive wardrobe in that one suitcase, but she was wearing what, in my male ignorance, I would call a dinner dress—not formal yet not for the street—a dark brown silky material that enhanced the bright gold of her hair. In a time when makeup is meant to look like no makeup I can't say what she had done to her face, but there was something new about her. She looked like a kid about to be taken to a party, which was exactly what I'd hoped for.

I offered her the Trapeze Bar, which is on the mezzanine above the lobby.

"It's noisy, crowded, but a place where you'll certainly meet someone you know," I said. I saw her face grow serious and I hurried on. "There's the Queen's Parlor—dim lights, soft whispers, for the romantically minded. Perhaps we should save that for another time? Then there is the Blue Lagoon, where they serve an early dinner for theatergoers, and where, if you like old show tunes, there is a piano player you won't believe."

"I love old show tunes," she said.

It would have been my choice, too. We went down to the lobby level and across the open area to the velvet rope that blocked the entrance to the Blue Lagoon. You don't get in there without a reservation. I have pull with the maitre d'. Mr. Cardoza looks like an elegant Spanish nobleman—and probably was in his youth. He took us to a table not too close to and not too far from the little bandstand where Jake Floyd presides at the baby grand piano. Television viewers will remember Jake as the man who made music for the Dick Thomas talk show, five days a week for years. Chambrun stole Jake away from Dick Thomas a while back and installed him in the Blue Lagoon. It was a ten-strike as far as business was concerned. People flock there from dinnertime until the early hours of the morning to catch his intervals at the keyboard. Jake says he started out playing a piano in a house of ill repute in New Orleans. The management posted a hundred bucks to be given to anyone who could name a tune Jack couldn't play.

"I had to know," Jake said, "because they didn't have a hundred bucks."

Jake is a wiry little man with a sandy fringe around his bald head. There is always a cigar in his mouth, even in an elegant room like the Blue Lagoon. He never lights it, but keeps rolling it from one corner of his mouth to the other. I think it's his security blanket.

Jake saw Cardoza bringing us to a table, nodded a greeting to me, and switched from what he was playing to "A Pretty Girl Is Like a Melody."

"You've been noticed," I said to Valerie.

A little flush of pleasure colored her cheeks. "He's marvelous, isn't he?" she said. She turned to Cardoza who was waiting for our drink order. "I'd like a very dry martini with a twist of lemon."

"On the rocks or straight up?" Cardoza asked.

"Straight up," she said. She knew her way around.

"The usual for you, Mr. Haskell?"

"Thanks, Luis." I am a one-drink man; one kind of drink. It is Jack Daniels on the rocks with a splash of plain water.

"It's a charming room," Valerie said, looking around.

"You've never been here before?" I asked.

"No. New York has never been a real stomping ground of mine. I was brought up in the Southwest—near Tucson. My father had a thing about New York. He hated it. I guess because I was born here, and by being born cost him my mother. He loved her very much."

"But Vassar was your college. That's just up the river in Poughkeepsie. No gay weekends in the big city?"

"I used to come down for theaters—Saturday matinees. This would have been far too fancy for me in those days."

"Your father could have bought the hotel for you if you'd asked for it," I said, meaning to keep it light. It didn't do what it was supposed to do. Fortunately the waiter brought our drinks and the dinner menu for us to study. I told him we'd order later—with the second drink.

"You'd probably think my father was strange about money," she said. "He'd been very lucky with it. Everything he turned his hand to worked, made him more and more. 'But you never know whether people like you for what you are or what you've got,' he used to say. When I began to grow up he worried about what it would do to me. He was sure every man I met would be after me for what I'd someday inherit, not just because I was . . . was attractive."

"Didn't he ever look at you?" I asked. "You'd never need money to attract men."

"Thanks, Mark. But I was never sure. My father used to say, 'Nobody is ever sorry for a girl on a yacht.' Would you believe that when I went to Vassar I was entered under my mother's name—Valerie

Hanson? My father convinced me that things wouldn't be normal for me if people knew I was the McCandless heiress.''

"You met your husband at Vassar, didn't you?"

I seemed to have a genius for turning the conversation to things that touched tender places. I saw pain in those dark, violet eyes.

She nodded. "Richard's education had been interrupted by Vietnam," she said. "He'd enlisted in the air force. When he got back he needed some extra college credits before going on to law school. He happened to choose Vassar—and later me. He had no idea I was a McCandless. He didn't know till after he'd asked me to marry him."

"It didn't turn him off," I said.

She laughed. "It almost did. But I persuaded him to go out to Tucson with me for the spring holiday, to meet my father. Dad was satisfied Richard wasn't a fortune hunter. They got along fine. Dad gave us advice that we followed. We were married, quietly, by a justice of the peace in Tucson. No publicity, no hoopla. Dad offered to help while Richard was in law school. He said any father-in-law with an ability to help would. Incidentally, before Richard died he'd paid back every penny my father had advanced us. We went to live in Ohio, and none of Richard's friends ever knew that I was a 'poor little rich girl.' Until . . . until afterward. Some reporter dug it up. I was suddenly a stranger—as though I'd cheated them out of some sort of juicy gossip for five years."

We ordered a second drink and I left the choice of dinner to Mr. Cardoza. Valerie was wound up about

herself and I was happy to let her go on. I sensed that
she needed to talk.

"I've been very bad luck for people I was close to,"
she said, "beginning with my mother whom I never
knew or saw. I . . . I was bad luck for my father. I cost
him the woman he worshipped. I...I was bad luck for
Richard."

"For God's sake, Valerie, you didn't set fire to the
hotel."

"I'm bad luck for people I get close to," she said.
"There was a girl at Vassar. We were good friends. She
disappeared out of my life when I married. One day,
after Richard, after I'd come to New York, I ran into
her on the street. Her name was Eleanor Payson. I
hadn't wanted friends, but I was delighted to find her
again. She was in big trouble. She'd been having an
affair with a married man. She'd borne him an illegit-
imate child, a little son—just two years old when we
met again. The man had gone haywire, it seems. He
was treating her badly, physically beating up on her.
She was afraid for the baby. She had no way to escape. She had no money. She was stuck. It was one
time I could use the money I now had to help someone I cared about. I rented a cottage for her out in
Tucson; I gave her money to live on for a while till she
could get on her own feet. I arranged for her to fly out
to Tucson with her child." Valerie looked away from
me. "I'm bad luck, Mark. That plane I put her on
crashed just a few miles short of Tucson. Everybody
on board was killed. It isn't healthy to have me for a
friend."

"Nonsense. What about the man?"

"I never knew who he was, what his name was. He never surfaced. There was nothing he could do. He had a marriage he hadn't been willing to give up for Eleanor. It wouldn't have done any good for him to reveal his connection with her then."

"So you didn't set the fire in which your husband died, and you didn't pilot the plane in which your friend died," I said. "You weren't responsible for the physical defects that caused your mother to die when you were born. You didn't know, had never laid eyes on, Carl Rogers, the man who was shot in your apartment last night. That's what you told Keegan, isn't it?"

"Yes. Because it's true."

I grinned at her. "So you see, you've got it upside down. You weren't bad luck for anyone. They've been bad luck for you."

She looked at me for a moment. Those deep, warm eyes. "You're a nice man, Mark," she said. "You've brought me to this charming place to take me away from my world of gloom and doom. So let's stay out of it."

She was right, of course, and so we did. We had our second drink. Mr. Cardoza provided us with a perfect summer dinner: a delicious cold vichyssoise, broiled Maine lobster, a salad out of a dream, a brandy-flavored mousse for dessert. Valerie and I talked about everything but her troubles.

In a break, Jake Floyd came down from the band-stand to our table. He has an eye for a pretty girl. She flattered him for his marvelous music, he flattered her by bemoaning the fact that I had found her first. She mentioned some old Cole Porter tunes she loved, and when he went back to his piano he played them all for her.

At some point the spell was broken for her and she asked me what Keegan had had to say about her.

"Not tonight," I said. "We'll have a 'gloom-and-doom' session the next time around. Keegan will soon be off in another direction. He's not as good an amateur psychiatrist as he thinks he is."

You can stay entertained in the Blue Lagoon for a long time. It was after eleven when I realized, reluctantly, that I had responsibilities.

"About this time every night," I told Valerie, "I take on the role of Marshal Dillon putting Dodge City to bed. It's my job to cover the other bars, restaurants, private parties, to make sure everything is functioning as it should. Care to make the rounds with me?"

"Oh, Mark, I don't think I . . ."

"There's a lot of night life you haven't seen."

"Do you know that I haven't had a wink of sleep since . . . since the night before last? It has been so wonderfully relaxing I think I could go out round the clock the minute my head hits the pillow. Perhaps another night?"

"My nights are yours as long as you want," I said. "I'll take you back to your place."

I said goodnight to her at the door of Five A, resisting the impulse toward a goodnight kiss. I threatened to call her before lunch the next morning and she didn't discourage me.

I went down to the mezzanine to visit the Trapeze Bar. It was crowded with after-theater drinkers. The room got its name from some Calder-type mobiles of circus acrobats on trapezes. The air-conditioning system keeps them in motion, like tiny, live people.

There were a couple of dozen characters I knew, and I worked my way slowly down the bar, saying hello, passing the time of night, listening to the latest wise crack from some Broadway wit. Then I saw Eddie, the bartender, signaling to me.

"Lady for you on the telephone, Mark," he said.

Without meaning to sound vain, I have to say it could be any one of a half-dozen ladies.

For a moment the voice on the phone was unrecognizable, strained, shaken.

"Mark?"

"Yes. Who is it?"

"Oh my God, Mark—it's Valerie."

"Val! What is it? You sound—"

"On the floor in my bedroom, Mark. Another one—"

"Another what?"

"A man—shot in the head! Oh my God!"

"Sit tight," I said.

It didn't make the slightest sense, couldn't be true, and yet she'd said it. I turned to Eddie.

"Get Jerry Dodd and Mr. Chambrun," I said. "Emergency in Five A." Jerry Dodd is head of hotel security.

"What do I tell them?" Eddie asked.

"It could be a homicide," I said, and took off.

It took me about three minutes to get to Five A. Valerie was standing just outside the door in the hall. As I reached her she grasped my hands in hers. They were ice cold.

"I—I didn't know what to do but call you," she said. "The switchboard operator said she could find you. I thought she never would."

We went into the suite together. The red-coated huntsman was still taking the same hedge on the same horse. The room was undisturbed, just as I had last seen it. Valerie seemed unwilling to go a step further.

"In the bedroom on the left," she said. She sounded almost strangled. I thought if she let go my hands her legs might just buckle under her. But she grabbed the back of an armchair and stood there, staring down the corridor toward the bedroom.

I told myself she'd cracked under the strain; it was a fantasy; there'd be no one in the bedroom.

But there was.

It was totally incongruous. The room wasn't in any kind of disorder. There were a few toilet articles on the dressing table, a silver-backed hairbrush, a tortoiseshell comb. The closet door was partly open and I could see a couple of dresses and a negligee hanging there. The bedside lamp was on, and the two lights on either side of the dressing table mirror were on. They worked from a switch at the door. Valerie must have walked down the little hall when I left her, stepped into the bedroom, switched on the lights, and seen what was lying on the throw rug beside the bed.

Dead men with gaping gunshot wounds in their foreheads are not an everyday experience for me. I felt a little wave of nausea sweep over me as I saw the dark pool of blood under his cheek. It was shocking, but, my God, what it must have been for Valerie! The second time in twenty-four hours.

I didn't need to examine the body to know there was
no need to try to get medical help. The whole left side
of the man's head was blown away. I couldn't tell if I
knew him or not. The side of his face that might be
recognizable was pressed against the bloodied rug. His
suit was a summer gabardine, tan; brown and white
sport shoes; a rather gaudy plaid sport shirt. His hair
was probably dark, but it was matted with blood on
the side I could see.

I didn't move. I just stood there, holding onto the
door jamb. Death isn't unusual in the hotel, any more
than it is in any other community. But this kind of violence was rare. I looked around for a weapon, a gun,
but there was nothing in sight.

I heard voices out in the living room and then footsteps coming my way. Jerry Dodd, our security chief,
is a wiry, intense little man, a former FBI agent, a
tough cookie, trusted to the very end of the line by
Chambrun. He stepped past me into the room.

"Jesus!" I heard him say, under his breath. Then he
turned to me. "You touch anything, Mark?"

"Just this doorpost I'm hanging onto," I said.

"The lady tell you her story?"

"Not yet. I spent the evening with her in the Blue
Lagoon. I brought her upstairs about twenty past
eleven. I went down to the Trapeze and the switchboard found me there. I came straight up—and
straight down the hall. You know—?"

"That this same thing happened to her last night?
Yes, I know. This is for the cops, Mark, not me. My
job is to see that nobody messes it up till they get here.
You better put in the call from the front room."

"I got word to Chambrun," I said.

"He'll tell you to call the cops, too," Jerry said.

I turned away and went back down the hall to the living room. Valerie was still standing there, gripping the back of the armchair. I told her I had to call the police. She didn't move or speak. She just stood there, staring down the empty hall.

The switchboard got me through to the local precinct and I was still reporting what we had seen when Chambrun walked in from the outer hall. He was wearing a dinner jacket with a red carnation in the lapel. He glanced at me and went over to Valerie.

"Mrs. Summers? I'm Pierre Chambrun."

She might not have heard him. She didn't move or speak. He turned to listen to what I was telling the desk sergeant at the precinct. Without another word he walked down the hall to the bedroom.

I came over from the phone and put my arm around Valerie. "You'd better sit down. This is going to be a long haul," I said.

She let me move her around to the front of the chair and lower her into it. Those wide, violet eyes stared up at me.

"Mark?"

"Yes."

"It is you, isn't it, Mark?"

"Yes."

"It is a dream, isn't it? A nightmare? I've left out going to sleep and dreamed all this?"

"I'm afraid not."

"Oh my God, Mark!"

I left my hand on her shoulder. "You're going to have to pull yourself together, Val," I said. "Chambrun is going to talk to you, and Jerry Dodd, our security man, is going to talk to you. Worse than that, the police are going to talk to you, far into the night."

"Lieutenant Keegan?"

"Since it's you, they'll probably think of it as his case. Can I get you something—a drink, order you some coffee?"

"Who is he, Mark?"

"I don't know. You don't know?"

"Mark, I came into the suite, went straight down the hall to the bedroom, switched on the lights, and...and there he was! I just got a glimpse of him. I ran out of there and to the phone. I didn't go back! I waited in the outside hallway for you."

Chambrun reappeared. He was the hanging judge, but I knew it wasn't aimed at Valerie. Disturb the orderly workings of his hotel and he is suddenly a dangerous enemy.

"There isn't anything we can do until the police come, Mrs. Summers," he said. "We can't touch the man or move him to try to identify him. I know this is a shock for you and it's not going to be easy. The first thing the police are going to ask you is how and where you spent your evening."

"I can answer that," I said. "I came up here at a quarter past six and invited Valerie for a drink and dinner. She went back down the hall to her room, changed, and then we went to the Blue Lagoon. We stayed there till a little after eleven. I had to make my rounds, I brought Valerie back up here, went down to the Trapeze and the switchboard found me there for her. She was never out of my sight in all that time— quarter after six till about twenty past eleven."

"A useful alibi," Chambrun said. "I don't suppose the man was there in your bedroom when you went to change."

"I don't believe you've asked me that, Mr. Chambrun!" she said.

"Keegan may find a lot more curious things than that to ask you," Chambrun said. "I can tell you one thing. He wasn't killed after Mark brought you up here at eleven-twenty. Blood's dried on the rug, early rigor mortis has set in. He's been dead for quite some time—hours I'd say."

"So the alibi does it—as if she needed an alibi," I said.

"You notice anything queer about the bedroom, Mark?"

"Aside from a dead man on the floor—no."

"The bed wasn't turned down," he said.

Valerie looked at him as if he was off his rocker. "I don't understand," she said. "The bed wasn't turned down?"

"Routine," he said. "The floor maid would normally come in about eight or eight-thirty to turn down your bed. For some reason she didn't come. Mark, call the housekeeper's room and ask her, or if she isn't there, the floor maid to come in here."

It was typical, I thought, for Chambrun to be concerned about a minor slipup in the hotel routine when we were confronted by a murder. Then I almost got down on my knees to apologize to him. Sure, he was aware of every detail of the hotel's operation, which is why he is so superlative at his job. In this case the detail he'd noticed could be very important. If the maid had come into Five A to turn down the bed at eight or eight-thirty and found the dead man, she'd have reported it at once. It would have helped answer the question of when it happened. If she had come in and he wasn't there, that would have told us something, too. The point was she hadn't come at all. Why? I thought I knew the answer even before I got the housekeeper on the phone.

Mrs. Kniffin is a motherly old biddy who supervises the housekeeping services on a half dozen floors. She'd been at the job for almost twenty years, totally reliable, almost frighteningly efficient. Luckily she was in the housekeeper's room on Five when I called in.

"Mr. Chambrun's down the hall in Five A, Mrs. Kniffin," I said. "Could you see him for a minute?"

"What's wrong?" the old gal asked.

"The night maid didn't turn down the bed in here," I said.

"Oh, for heaven's sake!" Mrs. Kniffin said. She sounded disgusted. "Be right there."

I crossed the room and rejoined Chambrun and Valerie. He was talking to her quite gently. "You're quite right to be frightened, Mrs. Summers," he was saying. "The same kind of violence happening to you two nights in a row is not acceptable as a coincidence. Not to me, at any rate, nor will it be to the police. You'll be in for a long and exhausting questioning. It's going to be very hard for them to believe that you can't explain or suggest an explanation for what's going on."

"But I don't know, Mr. Chambrun!" Valerie almost shouted at him. "The man last night I never saw before in my life. This man—I only just glanced at him—is a stranger. Last night there could have been a dozen explanations for how a man got in the wrong apartment, or why he was there deliberately. If he'd heard in the neighborhood that I was wealthy, he may have thought I'd have jewels or valuables. But this ... !''

"You're going to have to look at a lot of ugly facts, Mrs. Summers," Chambrun said. "There is someone missing, don't you see? The man last night didn't shoot himself and then dispose of the gun. We haven't searched the bedroom here, but there's no gun in sight. Missing is a killer, in both instances. Keegan is going to convince himself that there is no one missing, that the killer is you."

"But Mr Chambrun—!"

"There is a difference between this situation and the one last night," he said, in a flat, unemotional voice. "Someone had to be able to break into your apartment last night without leaving any trace of how it was done. You had the only key—except the superintendent and possibly the owner. Since the superintendent and the owner seem to be accounted for, Keegan chose to believe that you had some dealings with a drug and sex peddler."

"But I never—"

"It's different here," Chambrun said, not letting her interrupt. "Any number of people could get into this suite while you were dining with Mark. The maid *should* have gotten in. A bell captain or bellboy could get a key from the front desk. Maintenance would have a key for emergency purposes. I'm afraid Keegan won't be impressed. The simplest answer, to him, would be that you let the man in. That he was already in your bedroom, dead, when Mark stopped by to invite you out for a drink.''

"That I could go to my room and change my clothes with a dead man lying on the floor?" she asked, eyes wide as saucers.

"If you were cold-blooded enough to kill, Mrs. Summers, you would be quite capable of changing your clothes in the presence of a corpse."

"Oh my God!" she said, and covered her face with her hands.

There was a knock on the outer door and I went to admit Mrs. Kniffin. With her was a uniformed maid looking scared out of her wits. Mrs. Kniffin, starched and stiff, barged past me.

"You sent for me, Mr. Chambrun?"

He gave her an old-friend smile. "How are you, Gladys?" he said. He glanced at the maid. "This is Agnes Mueller. How is your family, Agnes? Is your sister doing well in school?"

What a man! He knows everything about everybody who works for him. That's why they would all die for him.

Mrs. Kniffin gave Valerie an unfriendly look. "What is this nonsense about the bed, Mr. Chambrun," she said.

"It wasn't turned down," Chambrun said.

Mrs. Kniffin looked at the frightened Agnes.

"There was a 'Do Not Disturb' sign on the door," the maid managed to say.

"I assumed that," Chambrun said, "but I just wanted to hear it from you. It's not going to be a secret for long, Gladys. A man has been killed in the bedroom. The police are on their way. I noticed that the bed hadn't been turned down and I simply wanted to know why." The two women looked frozen where they stood. Chambrun turned to me. "Was there a sign on the door when you called on Mrs. Summers at six-fifteen?"

"Positively not," I said.

"Did Mrs. Summers leave a sign on the door when you went out?"

"Of course not."

"And when you came back at eleven-twenty?"

"No sign," I said.

"If you think Agnes is lying about the sign..." Mrs. Kniffin said, hackles up.

"I don't think any such thing," Chambrun said. "Thank you both. The police will be asking you about this. Don't be frightened. Just tell them how it was, Agnes."

"Y-yes, sir."

"By the way, Agnes, what time did you come here to turn down the bed and see the sign on the door?"

"We do this hall about eight-thirty," Mrs. Kniffin cut in. "It could have been a little after; eight-forty, quarter to nine."

Chambrun nodded. "So at least we know when the killer was in here with his victim," he said. "Tell me, Agnes, did you see any strangers in the hall before that time, or later?"

"That's a silly question, Mr. Chambrun," Mrs. Kniffin said. She had been around long enough to take no nonsense, even from the Man. "There are no permanent residents on this corridor. We don't see anything but strangers."

Chambrun smiled at her and gave her a courteous little bow. "I stand corrected, Gladys. Tell me, Agnes, did you notice sometime later that the sign was gone?"

"No, sir," the maid said. "I'd finished with this corridor. I had no reason to check it out again. After I've turned down the beds I go to the housekeeper's room and wait for calls. Someone may need fresh towels or something. It's been a quiet evening."

"Not for much longer," Chambrun said, his smile evaporating.

The thundering herd was on us; cops, plainclothes detectives, police photographer, and a Black Irishman with a bitter look to him.

"I take it we don't need a court order for this, do we, Mr. Chambrun?" Keegan asked. "Where is it?"

FOUR

THERE IS SOMETHING almost grimly impersonal about the police in action. That "May I see your license, please," deadpan approach, indicating that there is no chink anywhere for sympathy or understanding to seep through. It's a technique, not inhumanity. A team from Homicide going to work has that blank-faced efficiency that has a way of letting you know that you can expect nothing but a hard time from them. Each of them knows exactly what to do; the man with the camera, the fingerprint men, the deputy medical examiner, the men searching the entire premises, in this case for a weapon. A uniformed cop guarded the door. None of us was free to leave Five A without permission from the man in charge, Lieutenant Keegan.

Chambrun was permitted to use the phone, and he spent quite a while in the far corner of the room, obviously making more than one call. Mrs. Kniffin and Agnes Mueller were huddled across the way from him, whispering together. I stood by Valerie's chair, my hand on her shoulder. I could feel her whole body trembling. If you minded your conversation being overheard there was nothing to talk about but the weather. Jerry Dodd had not reappeared, and I gathered he was giving Keegan's men a guided tour of the suite. There was a back way to the service area, another way in and out a killer could have used. The murderer could have gone that way, used the service elevator to go up or down, gotten rid of his gun on any one of forty floors—if he wanted to get rid of it. I had the uncomfortable feeling that Five A was about as accessible as Grand Central Station. Unless the doors, front and back, were locked and bolted on the inside it would be relatively simple to come and go if there was no one in residence to blow the whistle on you.

Chambrun came back from the phone and stood in front of Valerie, looking down at her.

"I've arranged to move you out of here as soon as Lieutenant Keegan is through with you, Mrs. Summers. We have a room on Twelve, and my secretary, Miss Ruysdale, will stay there with you. I've called Gardner Fails to tell him what's happened. He's agreed with me that you need a lawyer whose business is criminal cases. I've called a man I know, Andrew Lukens. He's on his way. I urge you to follow his instructions exactly, without any deviation."

"I . . . I don't understand why I need a criminal lawyer," Valerie said, her voice shaken.

"Because you are going to be a prime suspect, Mrs. Summers. I don't happen to think you are, you understand, but if I were Keegan I would have to prove it out. He'll be taking a statement from you. It shouldn't be very complicated. You left your suite here about six-thirty with Mark. There was no one here when you left. You spent roughly five hours in the Blue Lagoon with Mark; Cardoza, Jake Floyd, the waiter who served you, all witnesses to that. Mark brought you back up here, said goodnight to you at the front door. You came in, went down the hall to your bedroom, found the body, called Mark for help. You may not be able to prove what you did last night, but there are no ifs, ands, or buts about tonight. The man wasn't killed after you got back here from the Blue Lagoon. He'd been dead for some time."

"You thought I might have killed him before I went out with Mark," Valerie said.

Chambrun shook his head. "I thought Keegan might think that," he said.

"I'm very grateful, Mr. Chambrun." I could feel her relax just a little.

"I don't want to make things any more difficult for you than they are, Mrs. Summers," Chambrun said. "I told you earlier that I can't view this as a coincidence. Somebody is trying to turn your life into a gruesome nightmare. Who, Mrs. Summers? Who hates you? Who wants to harm you?"

She stared at him, eyes wide and frightened. "I...I don't have any friends, Mr. Chambrun. By the same token I don't have any enemies."

"I'm afraid I don't think so," Chambrun said. "Think!"

At that moment Keegan, followed by Jerry Dodd and a uniformed cop, came out of the bedroom section of the suite.

"I'm going to need a statement from you, Mrs. Summers," the detective said. "The rest of you I'll take, one by one, when I'm through with Mrs. Summers. Can you all wait for me in Mr. Chambrun's office?"

"I've arranged to move Mrs. Summers to Room 1216 when you're through with her, Lieutenant," Chambrun said. "My secretary, Miss Ruysdale, will stay there with her. Our security people will guard the hallway."

"That will depend on what she has to tell me," Keegan said. "Now, if you'll all go down to Mr. Chambrun's office . . ."

Valerie reached up and her fingers closed on my wrist, cold, desperate. "Please!" she whispered.

"I spent the entire evening with Mrs. Summers," I told Keegan. "It might save time if I stayed here with her. I can corroborate everything she'll have to tell you."

He gave me a tight little smile. "You can do your corroborating later, Mr. Haskell," he said. "Now, all of you, get moving."

I glanced at Chambrun for help, but he refused to look my way. I bent down and touched Valerie's cheek with my free hand.

"I'm sorry," I said. "See you as soon as I can."

She let go my wrist and lowered her head, making a little moaning sound.

CHAMBRUN AND Jerry Dodd and I, along with Mrs. Kniffin and Agnes, went down to Chambrun's office on the second floor. The two ladies seemed to need to use the plumbing facilities in Chambrun's dressing room, just off the office.

Chambrun went to the sideboard. There is a Turkish coffee maker there that Ruysdale keeps going for him round the clock. It's pretty vile stuff, I think, and nobody touches it but the Man.

"Anyone's entitled to a drink who wants one," Chambrun said, as he carried a demitasse over to his desk.

I went to the sideboard and poured myself a stiff slug of Jack Daniels. Jerry Dodd filled us in on some facts we didn't have.

"No gun," he said. "Not anywhere—so far. Keegan's got a couple of men searching the service area, top to bottom. Take him about three days if they want to sift all the trash cans."

"You don't have a high opinion of Keegan?" Chambrun asked.

"He's a mean sonofabitch," Jerry said, without emotion. "But he's a good cop. The boys in the district attorney's office love him, because when he presents them with a case it sticks. His middle name is 'Thorough.'"

"He comment to you at all about what he found in Five A?"

"He said, 'That crazy dame is at it again. This time we've got to put her away before she tries another time.' He's convinced about her, Mr. Chambrun, but he won't drop the net over her until he's got all the pieces together."

"Your opinion?" Chambrun asked, sipping his coffee.

"I don't have an opinion yet," Jerry said, "I don't have a handle yet to start with. I didn't pay much attention to what happened last night—in her Tenth Street apartment. Read the story in the afternoon *Post* when I heard she was here in the Beaumont. It could have been a robbery, a falling out between thieves, I thought. Or the lady could have had some kind of relationship with the dead man, rowed with him, and let him have it."

"And disposed of her gun, went to the theater, and didn't call the police for hours?" I said. "That's pretty far out."

"We don't know that she went to the theater," Chambrun said.

"You buy Keegan's theory?" Jerry asked the Man.

"I haven't bought anything," Chambrun said. "Not Keegan's theory, not Valerie Summers' story. Either way we have a psychotic killer operating here in the hotel. If the lady gets by this present inquisition we'll move her to 1216. Then we see to it, Jerry, that nothing more happens. Nobody that you don't know gets in to see her. We guard the hall, we watch her round the clock. This is our ball park and we keep it safe."

"Right," Jerry said. "I'll set things in motion."

"We're protecting the lady from someone, or someone from the lady," Chambrun said. "Whichever way it is, the buck stops here."

"Right," Jerry said, and took off.

Chambrun sat still, staring down at his empty coffee cup.

"You say we don't know if she went to the theater last night," I said. "But we do know that tonight she was with me for five solid hours. I'll swear there was no 'Do Not Disturb' sign on her door when we left at six-thirty, or when we got back at nearly eleven-thirty. She wasn't killing anybody at eight-thirty or after when Agnes saw the sign. She was with me, with Cardoza and Jake Floyd and a whole roomful of people to back it up."

"We don't know that she hadn't already killed the man when you called on her at six-fifteen," Chambrun said.

"What happened? Did he decide to hang out the sign for her before he went back in the bedroom and died?"

He glanced at me, his eyes cold in their deep pouches. His precious hotel had been bloodied. "The lady sold her story to you?" he asked.

"The 'lady,'" I said, exasperated with him for hanging onto Keegan's notions, "was in—what shall I say? Shock? Depression? A mood of 'gloom and doom,' she called it. Finding a dead man on the living room rug in her apartment brought back a chain of horrors to her. Her mother died giving her life. Her husband was burned alive in a hotel fire. Her only friend after that was killed, along with her infant son, in a plane crash. She feels she's bad luck for anyone close to her."

"Like the man who was shot in her apartment?"

"For God's sake, boss, she never laid eyes on him before!"

He gave me that patient schoolteacher look of his. "There are facts," he said. "And there is the background which may give a totally different coloration to what appear to be facts. I am walking down the street, I say, to get a little fresh air, or to buy an evening paper. But the fact is I am walking away from a bank I've just robbed. I'm walking, because to run would draw attention to me." His eyes narrowed. "If I told you I had cut a man's throat and hung his body from a lamppost on a city street would you find yourself turned off?"

"Your lecture is full of jokes," I said.

"It's no joke, Mark. I did just that. I cut a man's throat and hung his body from a lamppost. That's murder. Don't you feel impelled to turn me in?"

"For the sake of argument—if I was a good citizen I would."

"Ah, but the background," Chambrun said. "It was in the dark days, the occupation of Paris by the Nazis. A Nazi officer raped and then beat to death two young French girls. He set fire to the house where they lived and burned it, the bodies, and any evidence into a pile of gray ash. Go to the law with it? Go to the police with it? Useless. He *was* the law, he *was* the police. The Resistance made itself the law and I its agent. So I came at him out of a dark alley. We couldn't risk attracting attention with a gunshot, so I cut his throat. I hung his body from a lamppost because his monster friends needed to be taught a lesson, issued a warning. Have I lost any sleep over that in the last thirty-five years? Not one single blink of an eye, not one single twinge of conscience."

"Fascinating, but—so what the hell?" I said.

"The background gives a different coloration to the facts," Chambrun said. "Keegan thinks Valerie Summers may have killed two men. 'That crazy dame,' he calls her. So, maybe she did kill them, Mark, but we don't know the background so we don't have the means of seeing the true colors. She is the daughter of the late, totally ruthless, industrial giant, Jeb McCandless. The McCandlesses of this world have more enemies than friends. Someone—a group, a 'family' in the Mafia sense—wants to collect on an old debt.

Your Mrs. Summers is the collection point. Her money or her life. She kills—but it's self-defense.''

"Why doesn't she just go to the police?"

Chambrun shrugged. "Who knows? Without the background, who knows?"

"Maybe she has a million-dollar diamond," I suggested. "A gang of thieves is out to get it. She's protecting her rightful property. Her old man was rich enough to buy her a million-dollar diamond."

"So, last night, she catches a thief looking for her diamond, shoots him, and then refuses to tell the police the simple truth? And again tonight?" Chambrun leaned forward in his chair. "You want to believe she's innocent, Mark? Then you have to explain who the man is who kills two different victims in two different places where the lady lives—and why—and within twenty-four hours. Last night, on Tenth Street, there were several logical explanations: a simple robbery attempt and a falling out between thieves, a drug deal, a sex deal. But add tonight to that and it gets far more complex, much harder to just pick something out of the air. What am I getting at, Mark? Keegan is going after facts. I'm interested in background that will explain whatever facts he finds. Those registration cards we look at every morning? We need to fill out one on Mrs. Valerie Summers. We know her credit rating, but that's about it. Is she, in fact, a drug addict? Is she sex crazy? Is she psychotic? Paranoid? Is she a 'crazy dame' who should be locked away from the civilized world? Or is she being given a lesson in terror by someone who may fit any of those labels?"

"How do we find out?" I asked.

"*You* find out," Chambrun said. "You've made friends with her. In or out of balance, she trusts you. Maybe the answer is in Tucson where she grew up. Maybe it's in that small Ohio town where she and her husband lived. Maybe it's downtown in the Village. There can be a medical history somewhere. There can even be a police record somewhere that a very rich young woman could keep hidden."

"And she can be as clean as the proverbial hound's tooth," I said.

"Either way it is background that will color facts. Go after it, Mark."

"You want me to go traveling halfway around the world?"

"If it comes to that," Chambrun said. "Make that your job for the next stretch of time. We'll cover your regular routines for you."

The door to the office opened and a girl from the secretarial pool appeared trying to block the way to Lieutenant Keegan. I realized that Ruysdale was up in 1216, waiting for Valerie.

"I tried to tell this man—" the girl said.

"It's all right, Miss Madison," Chambrun said. "We can't expect ordinary courtesy from the lieutenant. He's a policeman."

"Screw your courtesy and your court orders," Keegan almost shouted. The Black Irishman appeared to have flipped his wig.

Behind the detective in the doorway, giving a pleasant little nod to Maggie Madison, the stand-in secretary, was Andrew Lukens, the lawyer Chambrun had sent for to take care of Valerie. I knew Andy Lukens from an earlier problem. I suppose he's looking at forty from just one side or the other. It was nearly two-thirty in the morning, but Andy didn't look like a man who'd had a long hard day, which was the way I felt. He was wearing gray slacks, a brown summer-tweed jacket, a navy-blue sport shirt without tie. He looked, I thought, like a young Henry Fonda, a gentle humor suggested in his eyes and at the corners of his mouth. He stood there in the doorway, filling a pot-shaped pipe from a plastic pouch, amused by the scene Keegan was playing.

"It would be nice if someone in this fancy whore-house would choose to cooperate with the law!" Keegan stormed.

"Cooperation is our trade name, Lieutenant," Chambrun said.

"Where are those maids?"

"Right next door in my dressing room," Chambrun said, pointing toward the far door. "You want them?"

"I'll talk to them there," Keegan said. "It will be a pleasure to question a witness who isn't being coached by someone!"

Keegan charged across the office and into the dressing room. I hoped Mrs. Kniffin and Agnes Mueller weren't going to be caught unprepared for a male visitor.

"Hello, Andy," Chambrun said.

"Hi, Mr. Chambrun," Lukens sauntered over to us, holding a lighter to his pipe.

"Thanks for coming so promptly," Chambrun said.

"Lady in distress—my pleasure," Andy said.

"What's with him?" Chambrun asked, nodding toward the dressing room door.

"Frustration," Andy said. "He likes to work over his witnesses before their lawyers appear on the scene. I've defended two other people involved in homicide cases he handled. He doesn't approve of the fact that anyone, guilty or innocent, is entitled to the best possible defense."

"You'll take Mrs. Summers as a client!"

Andy gave the Man his charming, boyish grin. "A lady that lovely I'll defend with my life," he said. "The best Keegan can do right now is arrest Mrs. Summers as a material witness in two homicides. I pointed out to him that I could then get her out on bail in something under five minutes."

"You've heard her story?"

"I've heard the story she gave Keegan about tonight," Andy said. "She spent the evening with you, Mark." His grin was aimed at me. "Lucky man. From Jerry Dodd I got the story about the 'Do Not Disturb' sign. I take it he'll get the same story from the ladies in the next room?"

"And I'll bear out the rest of it," I said. "No sign when I got there at six-fifteen. She didn't sneak a sign on the door when we left at six-thirty. No sign on the door when we got back there at eleven-thirty."

"Keegan thinks she killed her man before you arrived to take her out," Andy said.

"And who put the sign on the door after we left?" I asked.

"And why?" Chambrun said.

"Someone is framing the lady," Andy said.

"I had a feeling you were the right lawyer for her, Andy," Chambrun said.

"Right now Mrs. Summers is goggle-eyed with fatigue and, you might say, double shock," Andy said. "I've suggested to your Miss Ruysdale, who's up in 1216 with the lady, that she get some sleeping pills from the hotel doctor and that it be 'Katie bar the door' until noon tomorrow—or, rather, today. She's not in shape to make sense to anyone until she's had some solid rest. Two nights, two murders."

"Will Keegan let her alone that long?" I asked.

"If he wants a court order I'll get it. And he knows it," Andy said.

"If the lady's guilty?" Chambrun asked.

Andy's mouth tightened. "I'll stay with her through the first jury verdict, and the court of appeals decision," he said.

"Good man," Chambrun said.

"I have a problem," Andy said. "Facts about my client."

"Join the club," Chambrun said.

Which is how I got delegated to find out the truth, the whole truth, and nothing but the truth about Valerie McCandless Summers.

Unfortunately for my weary bones the evening didn't end just then. Keegan had to have his innings with me. I told my story of the evening about four times before he'd let me up. In the middle of that interrogation there was a call from Dr. Partridge, our hotel physician. The old man was in a nasty mood, too, having been gotten out of bed by Betsy Ruysdale. He'd taken some sort of sedatives or sleeping pills up to 1216, only to be refused entrance. Chambrun put his call on the squawk box so we could all hear.

"Looks like an army up there," Partridge told Chambrun. "Cops, couple of Jerry Dodd's men. I can't just hand over this stuff to someone else to give to a woman I haven't seen."

Chambrun told him to hang on and turned to Keegan. "The hotel doctor was prepared to give Mrs. Summers something that will let her sleep. They won't let him into the room."

"Too many people trying to help that crazy broad," Keegan said.

"She isn't going to be any use to you, Lieutenant, until she gets her brains unscrambled," Chambrun said. "She can be too tired to make any sense."

Andy Lukens gave Keegan his lazy smile. "There's one advantage, Lieutenant. If she's asleep she won't be trying to go somewhere else. She won't be scheming with her friends and her lawyer to make things tough for you."

Keegan was an angry man but he wasn't entirely brainless. "Tell the doctor to go back there," he said to Chambrun. "I'll give orders."

"Knock her out for ten, twelve hours," Doc Partridge told Chambrun.

"Go, friend," Chambrun said.

Keegan faced the three of us, Chambrun, Andy Lukens, and me. I guess he saw us as the enemy.

"You know who that sonofabitch is up there?" he asked.

"What sonofabitch up where?" Chambrun asked.

"The dead man! One of my cops recognized him. He's a character; a hawker for a massage parlor in the Times Square area."

"Hawker?"

"He brings in the customers off the street. 'Hawker'—a circus term. You know the difference between a massage parlor and an old-fashioned whorehouse, Chambrun?"

"'House of ill-repute,' my father used to call them," Chambrun said.

"The difference is," Keegan said, "that a massage parlor offers sex for both men *and* women. This Willie Bloomfield—that's his name—provides the customers with just the kinds of perversions they enjoy. Interesting people who wind up dead in this lady's quarters! A drug peddler, a sex peddler! I've come across some queer ones in my time. What happens? Does she get some kind of sexual climax out of killing people?"

I saw a little nerve twitch at the corner of Chambrun's mouth. It was ugly thinking. For my money it wasn't even worth considering.

"You're suggesting some kind of a monster, Lieutenant," Andy Lukens said, very quietly.

"What else?" Keegan said.

"Oh, I agree with you," Andy said. "We're dealing with a monster, but is it the lady or someone out to destroy her?"

"Too farfetched!" Keegan said.

"As the old saying has it, Lieutenant," Andy said, "'you go to your church and I'll go to mine.' There's a hell of a lot more to find out about this than two oddly related corpses. Same gun?"

"Ballistics will tell us," Keegan said, "but my guess is yes."

"Where is it?"

"There are so many places to hide it in this joint it could take us a lifetime to find it," Keegan said. "We could get lucky—I hope."

"Background," Chambrun said, as if he was talking to himself. He looked at me. I was getting my orders again.

It's strange what violence can do to the atmosphere of a familiar place. The Beaumont has been my home, my town, my own personal world for about fifteen years. I went to work for Chambrun the summer I graduated from college. I had planned to be a newspaper man. Helping the then P.R. man at the Beaumont was, I thought, just a stopgap for the summer. The whole slightly dizzy world of famous actors, Hollywood glamor queens, foreign diplomats, presidents, prime ministers, corporate tycoons, social bigwigs playing against a community of a hard working, highly efficient staff presided over by Chambrun, who instantly appeared to me to be a genius at what he did, wiped out any dreams I'd have of covering news stories for some hard-nosed managing editor. All the excitement I'd ever wanted was right here, within four walls, and by some miracle I was asked to stay on and be a permanent part of it. I had come to feel about the hotel the way Chambrun does. The murder of a cheap punk like Willie Bloomfield, who didn't belong in our world at all, was a personal affront. I couldn't begin to buy Keegan's theory that Valerie Summers was some kind of sex-crazed maniac. That meant, however, that somewhere, moving through our bars, our restaurants, our shops, and down our hallways and corridors, someone, someone Andy Lukens had called a "monster," was moving undetected, unsuspected, laughing at Keegan for trying to pin *his* crimes on Valerie. And, I wondered, wasn't that exactly what he wanted? Wasn't Valerie's face in the center of the bull's-eye of this monster's target? It was no coincidence, as Chambrun had said, that two men had been murdered in exactly the same fashion in two different places where Valerie was staying.

Who and why? The answers must be in Valerie's background if we had the wit to find them.

The first gray morning light was beginning to seep through the hotel's windows when Keegan was finally through with me. All I had to do, sensibly, was stagger down the second-floor hallway to my apartment and hit the sack. I was exhausted enough to do just that, but I didn't. The Beaumont was under attack, had been invaded and I just had to have a look, make certain that the regular machinery hadn't been jolted off the rails.

The person I really wanted to see was Mike Maggio, the night bell captain. Mike is a bright-eyed, dark-skinned, tough and very shrewd street kid out of Little Italy. Under Chambrun's guidance Mike had learned to say "Yes, sir" and "No, madam" and other polite formulas without their sounding like a foreign language, but he'd never lost his street-smartness at spotting a phoney. He was ideal for the night shift, because it is in the after-theater and early morning hours that there is a lot of transient traffic in our bars, restaurants, and the Blue Lagoon. I used to kid him and say that he was like a good watchdog whose hackles start to rise before the stray cat comes around the corner of the building. He has a feel for

mischief even before it begins to unfold. He can sense
the approach of someone who isn't a "Beaumont
person" even before they come through the revolving
doors from the street.

At quarter to five in the morning the cleanup crews
are at work in the lobby and in the closed bars and
restaurants. Mike Maggio was waiting out his tour of
duty, lounging near the Fifth Avenue entrance, chat-
ting with Waters, the night doorman. He was wearing
his dark-blue uniform with the Beaumont seal over the
breast pocket. He somehow made that uniform look
like a high-style sport jacket.

"You look like you've been watching TV all night,"
he said to me.

"How come?"

"Red eyes," he said.

"I'm pooped, friend," I said.

"But not in jail," he said. "Silver lining to every
cloud."

"Give with the gossip, Mike," I said.

He shrugged expressive shoulders. "You pays your
money and you takes your choice," he said. "Even
cops talk, you know? They've been sharing the business of searching the lady's original suite on Five, and
they're standing guard outside 1216 with Jerry Dodd's
boys. Those security boys talk to me. I'm supposed to
have an eye for sinister strangers."

"And?"

"The cops are convinced that your lady friend is a
homicidal screwball. Two in two nights! Jerry's persuaded his people that the lady's being framed. Nobody's got any proof of anything, so far."

"What about you?" I asked.

He gave me that sly, street grin of his. "I'm like you," he said. "She charms me out of my socks, so she has to be innocent. There are two things that might interest you, though. First, Willie Bloomfield who got creamed up in Five A, isn't a stranger to some of us. He used to be a pimp for call girls before he went into the massage parlor business. He tried to muscle in on this territory about five years ago. We gave him the bums' rush, after everybody had a good look at him. Willie couldn't be hanging around the Beaumont for five minutes without being spotted and escorted, physically, out into the night. The welcome mat was definitely not out for our Willie. But he got in, got up to Five A, and got himself killed without anyone noticing him."

"You must have been out of the lobby here from time to time."

"Sure, but there's always a security man on the job looking out for Willie's kind of undesirable. Elevator men knew him, most of my bellhop crew knew him. It isn't often a character like that gets by us. How did our Willie manage it? That's number one."

"And number two?"

"The lady has a friend who just turned up about an hour ago. Looks like the late Gary Cooper; cowboy hat, cowboy boots, skin like saddle leather. He asked for the lady at the desk and was told she was under sedation, guarded by the police till she slept it out. No way he could see her or call her room. He pulled out a roll of bills that would choke a hippopotamus, demanded a room. No luggage, you know? Atterbury, on the desk, told him we had none. He let himself be persuaded to call the Plaza down the Avenue. They were able to provide Mr. Paul Spector with a room."

"Does Chambrun know this?"

"If Jerry Dodd's gotten around to telling him. Jerry knows. The cops know. I guess they figured he'd be back when the lady wakes up. You see, he claims to be an old family friend. Heard the news about the murder on Tenth Street; couldn't reach her. Wanted to be helpful. Finally he found out she was here through Gardner Fails, and took the first plane."

"From where?"

"Tucson. The lady's old man had a spread of some sort down there, that was in the paper. She grew up in Tucson. This Spector guy is, or was, part of that setup. 'You tell Mrs. Summers,' he said to Atterbury, 'the minute she wakes up, that I'm here, ready to help any way I can.'" Mike grinned. "I've got to say I'd rather have that guy on my team than playing against me."

"Tough?"

"Strong and silent. I've got to add, Mark, I don't think the lady will look at you twice with Gary Cooper on stage."

I was too tired just then to care whether Gary Cooper got the girl or not. Later on it mattered.

IT SEEMED TO ME my head had only just touched the pillow when my bedside phone rang. I'd told them on the switchboard to give me an extra hour. A bleary-eyed look at my clock told me someone had goofed. I'd been called an hour earlier than usual. It was only seven-thirty. I picked up the phone—because I knew it would just keep on ringing till I answered—ready to have someone's scalp.

"Cool it, Mark," Ora Veach said. She's the chief operator on the board. "I am sorry to do this to you, but the boss wants you in his office—'at your earliest convenience' I think the phrase was."

"'Mine not to reason why, mine but to do or die...'"

"I'm of the hot shower school as opposed to the cold for waking up," Miss Veach told me.

Somehow I managed to shower and shave and get into some clothes, feeling thick fingered, in about twenty minutes. Chambrun's office is only a few yards down the hall. Miss Ruysdale is always in the outer office whenever the boss is working, no matter what time of day or night, but not this morning. Then I remembered she was up in 1216 with Valerie. I crossed the room and opened the door to the inner sanctum.

Chambrun was sitting at his desk, and across from him, long legs crossed, cowboy boots shining in the morning sunlight, was obviously Mike Maggio's Gary Cooper.

"This is Mr. Spector, Mark," Chambrun said. "We've just ordered some breakfast and I took the liberty of counting you in."

Spector stood up, towering over me, and damned near crushed my right hand with his.

"Pleasure," he said.

He wore his hat in the house, I saw, pushed back a little to reveal sandy-red hair. With my hand hurting, I thought there was something almost sadistic about his white, even-toothed smile.

"Mr. Spector manages the McCandless ranch in Tucson," Chambrun said. "I thought talking with him might save you a long trip."

"Valerie owns a ranch somewhere?" I asked.

"No, sir, she don't," Spector said in a Texas drawl. "Ol' Jeb McCandless's estate owns it. I ran it for Jeb before he died, and the lawyers have kep' me on." He gave me what I considered was a patronizing smile. "What would a pretty gal like Val do with a cattle spread?"

"She could raise her own beef?" I said.

"She jes' collects the profits," Spector said.

"I've tried to bring Mr. Spector up-to-date," Chambrun said. "I've told him the line the police are following, and that we are working on other angles."

"Get my hands on that cop," Spector said, "and I'll break his damn neck. Val killin' a couple o' creeps? How crazy can you get?"

"Just that crazy, according to Lieutenant Keegan," Chambrun said.

"Damn fool," Spector said.

"To think of Mrs. Summers as a killer? Perhaps," Chambrun said. "But one thing is certain. If she isn't, then someone out of her past somewhere is out to destroy her. You said you were prepared to do anything you could to help her. Tell us what you can about the Tucson aspects of her life. She grew up there? Lived there with her father till he died? Or was it just till she got married?"

I learned later that it wasn't Spector who had hunted Chambrun down. When Jerry Dodd let Chambrun know that the king of the cowboys was at the Plaza it was the Man who got to him. "Time," Chambrun said later, "was vital. There was a killer loose who might strike again."

"People say I don't look it," Spector said, after a moment of silence, "but I am forty-five years old." He waited for us to comment on the miracle of his youthful looks, and when we didn't he, so help me, proceeded to roll a cigarette for himself. Cowboy right out of a movie, I thought. "I went to work on the McCandless spread when I was eighteen," he said, squinting at us through the smoke from his cigarette, which he got going by snapping an old-fashioned kitchen match into flame with his thumbnail. "That was twenty-seven years ago, and Val was jes' a baby, jes' three years ol' the first time I saw her. All golden an' shinin', even then. Ol' Jeb McCandless was kind o' mixed up about the kid, I guess. She was his daughter an' he was supposed to love her. But she'd stole his precious Georgie from him by bein' born. His wife's name had been Georgiana, but they called her Georgie. But the ol' man got to love Val as she grew up. Sometimes toward the end I thought there was somethin' almost—almost indecent about it. That's not the word I want..."

"Incestuous?" Chambrun suggested.

"Yeah...father dreamin' the wrong dreams about his daughter. You could see it in his eyes when he was lookin' at her without her knowin'. Not thinkin' about her like a daughter at all."

"I'm sure he hasn't come back to haunt her," Chambrun said. He sounded impatient. He's not a patient man before breakfast. "There were, of course, men in Valerie's life."

Spector flicked the ash from his homemade cigarette. He was smiling at the past somewhere. "Can you imagine what she was like ten, twelve years ago?

Eighteen, twenty? I want to tell you, Chambrun, they buzzed around her like bees after the queen. It wasn't because she was goin' to be one of the richest girls in the world. She was young, and alive, and beautiful, and—and hot stuff!''

"Are you saying she was promiscuous?" Chambrun asked, looking down at his well-manicured fingers.

"Hell, no," Spector said. "She was real choosy, but she had plenty to choose from. Older men, young men, teenaged boys. You could almost hear 'em sweatin'." He laughed. "You're gonna ask me so I'll tell you. I was one of 'em. I hankered after her till it hurt, way down inside. Still do, I guess."

"But you never got lucky?"

Pale blue eyes narrowed. "I should tell you that's none of your business, Mr. Chambrun. But in the circumstances—so you don't keep askin' yourself over and over—there was a moment in time when I thought I had it made. I didn't want the ranch, or ol' Jeb's money. I jes' wanted Val. It was the night before she went off East to college. I invited her to picnic up at the lake. It's a beautiful spot, high up, on the ranch. There was a moon, a soft, warm night. I told her how I felt, what I wanted. For a moment or two she let me touch her. We jes' about made that connection that sets off the rocket. You know what I mean? An' then she turned off." Spector drew a deep breath and let it out in a sigh. "The moment never came again. She went off to college, an' there she found someone else."

"Richard Summers, the man she married?" Chambrun said.

"There was someone else the first year," Spector said. "A professor fellow; taught literature of somethin'. Name of Newton, I think. I never saw him, but ol' Jeb told me about it. I think he knew what I was dreamin' and he wanted me to be let down easy. I got the message, and when Val came home that summer we never got back to where we left off. Then, the next year there was Dick Summers and Val was off to what she really wanted."

"You got to know Summers?"

"Oh, sure," Spector said. "I suppose Val could have run off somewhere with Dick Summers, married him, and told her ol' man about it later. She didn't. She's a square shooter. She brought him out to Tucson in the spring vacation. Ol' Jeb had one bee that was always buzzin' in his bonnet. Somebody was goin' to sweep his little girl off her feet for her money and not because of the person she was." He smiled at the past again. "Dick Summers was a good kid. I shouldn't call him a kid, I guess. He'd been through two years in Vietnam, which was a quick way to grow up. He was twenty-five that spring, be damn near thirty when he finished his education and got out of law school. That's startin' a career later than most, but it didn't bother Dick. That's what he wanted to do, that's what he was goin' to do. He didn't want help. He had veteran's benefits, and Val could get a job!" Spector laughed. "Ol' Jeb damn near split a seam when he heard that, but he approved. He'd persuaded Val to use her mother's name—Hanson—when she went to Vassar, so people wouldn't be suckin' around her for her money. Dick Summers was too good to be true. In June, when college was over, Dick came out to Tucson and he and Val were married. Simple ceremony, justice of the peace, no family, no relatives or friends, no announcement to the papers. Jes' two witnesses; me and Mrs. Renfrew who kept house for the ol' man. I kissed the bride, and I never saw Val again until she came back to Tucson for the ol' man's funeral. Dick didn't come with her then. He was tryin' a case in court, she told me. But I could see the marriage had worked out jes' fine. When we heard last year that Dick had died in a fire it was hard to believe. I tried to get in touch with Val, but she'd left Jeddo, the town in Ohio where they lived. Gardner Fails, the ol' man's lawyer knew where she'd gone, of course, but he'd promised her to keep it under his hat. Then yesterday I heard on TV what had happened in her apartment on Tenth Street. I tried to reach Fails, couldn't get him, and hopped the first plane I could get. When I hit the airport around two A.M. I called Fails again, and he tol' me there was a second murder and that Val was stayin' here at the Beaumont. So I came here.''

Chambrun looked up, his eyes hooded. ''You'd had no contact with Mrs. Summers for five years, except for the funeral of her father, yet when you heard what had happened you were out of the starting gate like Man o' War.''

Spector recrossed his long legs. ''The ol' man was my friend, my good friend. He left things so that I'm fixed good for keeps. His kid was in trouble!''

''And you still have a yen for her,'' Chambrun said.

Spector's cold, white smile widened. ''I'd be lyin' if I said I didn't. I've never got over that gal, but I don't expect anythin' except to be of use to her. That crazy cop gets tough with her and I'll pull out his arm by the roots and beat him to death with it.''

"Pretty picture," Chambrun said. He kept glancing at the far door and I knew he was thinking about breakfast. "You skipped pretty quickly over the professor at Vassar whose name, you say, was Newton."

"I never saw him," Spector said. "Val talked about him, that summer after her first year at college. I could tell she thought she was in love with him. Older man, opened up the windows to new things in her life: literature, art, music—I don't know. Stuff I didn't glom onto." Spector frowned. "Something bad happened to him, I think."

Chambrun seemed to perk up. "Bad?"

"I don't know what it was," Spector said. "That next winter, when Val was back at Vassar, the ol' man mentioned that something bad happened to 'that professor friend of Val's.' 'We're a hell of a lot safer out here than we'd be in New York, with all their cops,' he said. 'That professor friend of Val's got mugged. Crippled for life, according to the radio.' That's all. I never heard anymore about it. It was jes' a news item. Val had already found Dick Summers.''

Chambrun sat forward, suddenly intent. "*Derek* Newton? Was that his name, Derek Newton?"

"Dirk, or Derek—somethin' like that," Spector said.

Chambrun leaned back. "The people who touch Mrs. Summers' life really *are* unlucky," he said. He glanced at me. Derek Newton was someone we knew here at the Beaumont. He was—or had been—an attractive young man, scholar, teacher, who wrote—and still does—brilliant and witty book reviews for the

Sunday book sections and the more sophisticated literary-type magazines. He used to be a regular in the Trapeze Bar, stopping by two or three nights a week. He'd sit at a corner table and in ten minutes there'd be eight or ten people gathered around. Derek had revived the art of conversation. Three years ago the sky fell in on him. He'd been visiting some friends down in the Village. He was out on the street looking for a cab a little after midnight. He was brutally mugged. It was so senselessly brutal the cops thought it might be some personal grudge, even though a few bucks were stolen. Derek couldn't help them. He had no enemies, he told them. He had trouble enough reorganizing his own life. His spine had been injured and he was paralyzed from the waist down, confined to a wheelchair for the rest of his life. He was blinded in one eye, the side of his face crushed by that famous "blunt instrument." No more public appearances. No more rap sessions in the Trapeze Bar. He didn't want to see old friends, but he'd talk on the phone. I called him every few weeks, just to say hello. It didn't stop his reviewing and writing for the papers and magazines, but a charming and attractive young man simply vanished from public view. I remembered now that he'd delivered a series of lectures at women's colleges—Vassar, Barnard. So our Valerie, in her freshman year at Vassar, had taken a header for Derek. He'd been a real charmer back then.

Chambrun was right. It wasn't lucky to have been associated with Valerie McCandless. First her mother, then a man she'd had a crush on, then her husband, then her closest woman friend, and then the murder of two punks she may or may not have known. Varying degrees of violence in all the cases; no wonder she felt hounded by misfortune.

The special chef who handles Chambrun's breakfast appeared at that moment with a wagonload of goodies. I wasn't particularly interested in watching our cowboy friend eat what he'd ordered—juice, a sirloin steak, hashed brown potatoes, and a mound of toast. The prospect was somehow oppressive, and I knew what my cue was. Derek Newton might have something important to add to the saga of Valerie McCandless Summers.

FIVE

IT IS PAINFUL to invade the privacy of someone like Derek Newton. He was a man who loved people, had used his physical as well as his intellectual charms to attract them, and who now felt repulsive; felt that people only presented themselves because they felt sorry for him. He may have had close friends who'd gotten around that obstacle, but I wasn't one of them. The one contact with the outside world in which none of his troubles showed was in his writing. It still had all the wit and probing cleverness it had always had.

Derek wasn't eager to see me until I told him why I needed to talk. "Dear God, not another one!" he said when I called him. He hadn't heard the news about Willie Bloomfield. "I don't know how I can be useful. Valerie was a—a moment, long ago. But I know so little."

It wasn't quite ten in the morning when I reached his place. Valerie would be asleep for at least another two hours according to Doc Partridge.

Derek lives in a modern apartment building with elevator service. He has to because of his wheelchair. It is an attractive, lived-in looking place; books, paintings, an elaborate hi-fi set, and a view of the East River. He was ready when I arrived, having left his door unlocked for me. He just called out for me to come in when I knocked. I suspected he wanted to be set somewhere, not wheeling awkwardly around. He was actually sitting behind a flat-topped desk, his useless legs hidden. He wore large shell-rimmed black glasses. His left eye was, I gathered, a mangled mess. No cosmetic repair had been possible. Living with it had taught him little tricks. He'd learned how to sit so that you saw only the good side of his face. His smile was still as warm and friendly as it had been in the old days.

"This is a shocking business, Mark," he said. "There's coffee in that percolator on the sideboard if you'd care for some." He'd already poured a mug for himself. "How is Valerie bearing up?"

"She took the first one very well," I said, getting myself coffee. He gestured to a comfortable armchair across the desk from him. He'd placed it so that I was only looking at his good side. "The second one last night did her in. The doctor's sedated her and she's finally getting some sleep. Cops have been rough." I sat down.

"It just doesn't make any sense," Derek said. "Two total strangers!"

"The cops aren't sure of that. That's why I'm here, Derek. We need to find out everything we can about her past, her early beginnings—friends who might hold some kind of grudge against her. Because unless she's lying through her teeth someone is trying to punish her for something."

"Why did you think of me?" Derek asked.

I told him about our Tucson cowboy. "He seems to think you and Val had something going for a while. Even if you didn't, you knew her 'when,' as the saying goes."

He sat very still for a moment, his face turned away to look out the window at the river. "There was a time," he said finally, "when I had them lying at my feet like new-mown hay. Girls. They tend to develop crushes on the teacher. I was a guest lecturer at Vassar when I first met Val. There were a couple of dozen of them who had their eye on me. I was an attractive 'older man.' Would you believe twenty-six?" He turned his face and smiled at me. "I could have had my pick. I could have, and I did."

"Valerie?"

"No. No, not Valerie. She was a beautiful, young, fresh, lovely, delightful girl, and she offered it all to me, and I said a polite, if regretful, no thank you. I had my eyes—both of them in those days—focused somewhere else."

I suggested I found that hard to believe.

"Chemistry," he said. "There's no explaining chemistry, is there? This other one had it all for me. The morality rules in a girls' college today date back to 1910, but the behavior patterns are strictly the 1970s. A teacher who had an affair with a student would be tarred and feathered and ridden out of town on a rail in 1910. Today, unless you are blatantly indiscreet, nobody pays much attention. Poor Val— poor me. She wanted something to happen with me so much, but I wanted something else. The gal I wanted was all involved with someone else. Didn't have the time of day for me. Maybe that's what attracted me. Hard to get."

"But Valerie wouldn't have been?"

"Not for me she wouldn't. She wasn't just a little tramp, you understand. She was single-minded. What made it tough for her was that the girl I was interested in was her close friend.''

I felt a little jolt of electricity run along my spine. "Eleanor Payson?" I asked.

His smile vanished. The visible side of his face turned rock hard. "You psychic or something?" he asked.

"Val mentioned her," I said, "but not you."

"Did she mention what happened to Eleanor?"

"Plane crash, a few months ago," I said. "It was one of a chain of disasters to people Valerie cares about—her husband and her friend in the space of a few months. She's developed the morbid notion that she's bad luck for people who get close to her."

"She was trying to help Eleanor out of trouble," Derek said. "She was a good friend. It wasn't her fault that the landing gear on the plane malfunctioned, and that it crashed and burned when the pilot tried to land with his wheels up. Did Val tell you where Elly was going and why?"

"Sketchy," I said. "She told me Eleanor was having some problems with her love life; Valerie had arranged a place for her to go, helped her with money, I gathered." It was up to Derek to fill out the sketch if he wanted to.

"This happened to me just over three years ago," he said, after a pause. He brought his hands down on the metal arms of his wheelchair. His face, a muscle working along the line of his jaw, was turned toward the window again. "You know me! Old Joe Hopeless! I never got Elly to buy what I had to offer. I wanted her to marry me. I wanted her forever. I never got to first base. I wasn't even able to be a friend."

I could tell it hurt him. "Another guy?" I asked.

"Always another guy," he said, bitterly. "Always the same other guy. Would you believe, a married man, having an affair with a college girl? He never showed up where she was; she always went to him. The last time I saw her—would you believe it was the night this happened to me?—she was pregnant with his kid. She was determined to go through with it, to have the child, even though he wouldn't budge out of his marriage."

"Nice guy," I said. "Who is he?"

"I have no idea," Derek said. "If I did I just might kill him if I could get at him."

"Valerie suggested Eleanor was trying to get away from this guy."

"She died, keeping his identity a secret!" Derek said. "Wouldn't tell me. Didn't tell Val."

"You know that from Valerie?"

"Yes."

"Then you've seen Valerie since the plane crash?"

"No." He turned the rock-hard good side of his face to me. "The whole bloody thing is out of some kind of romantic horror novel," he said. "Did you know that Val went to Vassar using her mother's maiden name? Valerie Hanson, she called herself. None of her friends, nor I, knew that she was Jeb McCandless's daughter. Some crazy idea the old man had that all that money would produce some kind of unhappiness for her. I didn't know till a few months ago who she really was. The story came out in the papers when her husband died in that fire. I knew Dick Summers. It was a good marriage, with a few million bucks kept in hiding, for God's sake. I never saw her in that five years her marriage lasted. I have to admit I didn't even think about her. I had my own problem, a craving for Eleanor that never let up. But the night before Eleanor took off on that last plane trip she called me. She told me she'd run into Val, and that Val was helping her get away. She'd keep in touch, she promised."

"You didn't see her before she left?"

"Looking like this?" he said, angry, bitter.

I waited for him to go on.

"That night—that's what I call it, 'that night'—I went to see Eleanor. It was against the rules. I might interrupt her monster-man at his pleasure. But I'd called her on the phone, and she was suddenly in tears, and she told me she was pregnant, that her man didn't see that as a reason to change his pattern. I went down to Jane Street in the Village where she had an apartment. I pleaded with her to come away with me. I'd raise this other guy's child if she wanted to have it. I had the feeling she was being banged around by this bastard. But she wasn't having any. He was 'my man,' thick or thin, good or bad. I left her, walked a block toward the subway station, and—had my brains beaten out by some madman who obviously needed whatever money I had for a fix. Six months in a hospital and a nursing home; six months trying to get my life put together."

"Were you robbed?"

"Whatever I had. Fifteen or twenty bucks, a good wristwatch, wallet with credit cards and a driver's license."

"You didn't connect what happened to you with Eleanor's monster-man?"

"Oh, sure," he said, sounding suddenly tired. "But I had no idea who he is, was. I never told the police where I'd been. Said I'd gone to call on friends who were out."

"Why?"

"It could have gotten Eleanor in trouble with her man. I've spent the time since I got rolling again trying to identify him, but no dice. I've never found anyone who saw her with someone. Five, six years they were involved, but it was evidently so private, so hidden."

"But Eleanor called you, told you Val was helping her get away?"

He nodded. "She called me from time to time. Of course what had happened to me was in the papers, on the tube, everywhere. Once I suggested to her that it might have been her man who saw me coming out of her apartment and clobbered me. Not possible, she assured me. He was out of town 'on business' that night. She—she was listed among the casualties the morning after that plane crashed; she and the kid. She'd had a boy child. I...I managed to locate Val and talked to her on the phone. She was, you might say, in shock. She offered to come and see me, but I...I don't see people. There was nothing any of us could do—at least that mattered too much. Val took care of what are laughingly called 'the arrangements'—funeral for Elly and the baby boy. Elly had no family. Monsterman never surfaced." He drew a deep breath. "But you didn't come to see me to hear all this."

"I don't know what I came to hear, Derek," I said. "The detective investigating these two killings, one in Valerie's apartment and the one last night at the Beaumont, has both barrels aimed at her. The man killed in her apartment two nights ago, Carl Rogers, was a drug peddler and a porno dealer. Willie Bloomfield, who was shot in her room at the Beaumont last night, was in the sex business, managed a massage parlor. Keegan—that's the cop in charge—thinks Valerie may be a drug addict, a sex-queer of some sort. Would you buy that!''

"Oh, for Christ's sake!" Derek said.

"We need to know all we can about her past to knock that theory in the head," I said. "Our Tucson cowboy—Spector his name is—used an unfortunate phrase about her. He said she was 'hot stuff.' Is that how you thought of her when you first saw her at Vassar?''

He reached out, almost zombielike, for a package of cigarettes on his desk. He was looking back, remembering. He'd seen her first—what, eight, nine years ago?

"It can be a kind of fascinating, clinical study—a man teaching in a girls' college," he said. "I didn't live in Poughkeepsie where the college is. I was a guest lecturer. I drove up from New York on a Wednesday morning, lectured to three classes that afternoon, spent that night in a motel, lectured again on Thursday morning, drove back to the city after lunch. I was part of the community just one night a week. That kind of schedule suggests the possibility of a series of one-night stands."

"Is that how it was?"

He shook his head. "My code of ethics is, God help me, a little closer to 1910 than 1970. There was something about those college girls, coming there as freshmen at sixteen, seventeen. They were like flowers, just opening up. Oh, I suppose some of them had been screwing around in high school. You ever hear the figures on high school pregnancies? Scare the hell out of you if you had a daughter of your own. Anyway, sex was a major sport for many of them, away from home restrictions for the first time. I could have had a different one every Wednesday night if I'd wanted. I was an old-fashioned prude, I guess. I wanted more than fun and games; I wanted it to matter."

"Valerie could have been a Wednesday night gal?" I asked, trying to get him back on my course. "From what our Tucson cowboy says, I get the idea she was an old hand at it."

"Your Tucson cowboy is full of it," Derek said. He hesitated. "I haven't any right to tell you this, Mark, but if she's in trouble..."

"She could be," I said.

"One Wednesday afternoon, after my last lecture of the day, Valerie fell into step beside me as I walked across the campus to where my car was parked. It wasn't unusual for one of the students to join me, to discuss some point I'd just made in the lecture.

"'I'd like to discuss something rather personal with you, Mr. Newton,' Val said to me that day. You notice she called me *Mr.* Newton. 'I'd be very pleased,' she said, 'if you'd like to make love to me.'"

"Just like that?"

"Just like that," Derek said. "I have to tell you I was a little winded. I muttered something about being flattered, but... She broke in quickly, 'I have to tell you that it would be a first time for me, Mr. Newton. I understand that virgins aren't much fun the first time or two, but I'd try to learn quickly to please you.' I tried to think of some not unkind way to back off. I wasn't inclined to be an educator in that field, and, anyway, I'd already seen the girl I really wanted."

"Eleanor Payson?"

He nodded. "I tried to tell Val how pleased I was to have been asked, thought of, but that I was committed in another direction. She was embarrassed, probably hurt. She was sorry to have been so bold, but she hadn't known any other way. That was it, Mark; all there was then, all there was ever. But if your cowboy thinks she was 'hot stuff,' having it with the boys in Tucson, he's wrong. She'd waited till then to choose just the right person and I slammed the door on her. After that summer vacation she came back to college, met Dick Summers, and that was that. She made a good choice. He was older by a few years, been through a war. He was a man, a good one. I have no idea what went on in her marriage, but it seems to have worked."

"No kids," I said. "Five years and no kids; small-town married couple where kids are the rule, not the exception."

"I think they'd have had kids soon," Derek said. "Dick wanted to make it on his own, repay old Jeb McCandless for his help, before he took on new responsibilities. I think they were planning."

"What about drugs?" I asked.

"Oh, boy, Mark, I can't really answer that one. Those kids, a few years back, smoked pot the way my father used to smoke cornsilk. It was the smart thing to do. I have to think most of them tried it, anyway. But a big habit? A few went on, I suppose, to the really dangerous stuff. In the two years I knew Val at Vassar I never saw any signs that she was into anything like that. After Dick Summers came on the scene she just blossomed. It was pretty to see. I often regretted that I hadn't been the one to make it happen. You see, I never got what I wanted."

"Could Keegan be right?" I asked. "After she was tragically widowed could she have blown her stack? Taken to drugs, promiscuous sex?"

"I can't answer that, Mark," Derek said. "I haven't known her for the last five years. I can say there was never any gossip about her. If she's still the girl I knew back at Vassar I'd give you a prompt no. But is she still that girl today? I don't know, Mark. I just don't know."

IT WAS ALMOST NOON when I left Derek Newton and headed back for my home base. Chambrun had said something about someone else handling my routines while I went after "background," but whatever he'd had in mind had not involved the worlds of the press, the radio, and television. The lobby of the Beaumont was swarming with gentlemen and ladies from those worlds, frustrated and angry. They'd been treated to a "no comment" from Keegan, from Chambrun, and from my office. When I came in from the street they swarmed over me like buzzards after fresh meat!

I could only give them square one. Yes, there had been a second murder. Yes, it bore a grim likeness to what happened on Tenth Street the night before. Yes, the lady was in Dr. Partridge's care and couldn't be interviewed. No, I couldn't tell them if Keegan had any leads. I had no intention of making the lieutenant's fancy dreams public. That was up to him.

I noticed Eliot Stevens, the International Press man, loitering on the fringe of the demanding army. He is a sandy-haired guy, looking professional behind horn-rimmed glasses. He and I were old friends, and I realized he was waiting to get at me alone. I gave him a "thumbs-up" sign and he read it correctly. He sauntered over toward the elevators and I knew I'd find him waiting for me in my second-floor office.

When I finally got free of the outraged media I went into the private office behind the front desk and called Chambrun's office. Maggie Madison was still substituting for Ruysdale, and she told me Chambrun was in a session with the owners, who'd called an emergency meeting when the news of a murder within the Beaumont's sacred portals had broken. He couldn't be disturbed unless it was an emergency. I had nothing to tell him except that I had nothing to tell him.

Not knowing what was going on in 1216 and not wanting to ring that room phone in case Valerie was still resting, I took a quick elevator trip. I was surprised to see just one obvious plainclothes cop sitting near the door of 1216. The floor maid's cleaning wagon was standing just outside the open door of the room. I told the cop who I was.

"I heard there was an army up here," I said. "Just you?"

He told me he was Sergeant Polansky, one of Keegan's crew. "The lady's gone out," he told me.

"Gone out?"

"She and her lawyers and two cops to guard them," Polansky said. "Brunch somewhere in the neighborhood. They went out by the service elevator to avoid the press. I'm just here to see that no one with no business there goes into the room while she's gone.''

"The maid's in there?"

Polansky shrugged. "She had the right number of mops," he said.

"When do you expect Mrs. Summers back?" I asked.

He gave me a twisted little smile. "It could be quite a while," he said. "They're going to need to do a lot of planning. Keegan's going to nail that lady to the barn door. You can count on it."

Keegan wasn't out to solve a crime, I thought. He meant to prove himself right, no matter who got hurt. There was a nagging little thought that went with that idea. Could he be right? Could tragedy have turned a nice girl into something unbelievable? My job I told myself, was to prove it hadn't. And yet that wasn't my job, really. My job was to see to it that Beaumont was damaged as little as possible by the hoopla of a murder. If in the process I could clear Valerie Summers and ride off into the sunset with a lovely lady in front of me on my saddle horn, fine.

Eliot Stevens is a chain smoker, and there were already three cigarette butts in the ashtray on my desk when I finally got there. He didn't look like a man in a hurry.

"I'm willing to wait for *the* story," he said. "My colleagues, to coin a phrase, may be satisfied with just any story."

"I don't really have a story for you, Eliot," I said. "Nothing you don't already know. A drug peddler named Carl Rogers was shot to death in Mrs. Sum-

mers' Tenth Street apartment night before last. Her
lawyer brought her here as a safe place to stay. Last
night a porno-sex peddler was shot to death in her
room here. She claims she never laid eyes on either
man before. Off the record, Keegan doesn't believe
her."

"It's Keegan's kind of case," Eliot said, his long
legs stretched out in front of him, head tilted back as
he blew a smoke ring toward the ceiling light.

"How do you mean?"

"Ambitious man," Eliot said. "Married to the assistant commissioner's daughter, headed for high
places. You don't make a reputation on street-corner
shoot-outs. He's got everything here: dope, sex, a
beautiful rich lady, daughter of a famous corporate
giant—names, scandal." Eliot smiled at me. "Someone might even write a book about it."

I smiled back at him. "I'm making notes," I said.

"He suspects Mrs. Summers?" Eliot asked.

"Off the record. What makes you think he might?"

"It's the way his mind would work," Eliot said.
"Where the glamor lies, there lie headlines."

"You sound as if you don't like him."

"I don't, but I'll have to give you an honest evalu-
ation. I've covered half a dozen cases of his. You noticed he's always dressed for the camera, right out of
a custom tailor's shop? Always thinking of the big
story in which he'll be the key figure. But I have to tell
you this, with some reluctance. If it doesn't pan out
the way he wants it to, the way that will give him big
headlines, he'll keep after it until he gets the real killer. His score on success is pretty fabulous. If your
Mrs. Summers can survive his first attack, if it isn't the

way he hopes it is, she can count on being cleared beyond any doubts, because Keegan will come up with the real killer. He's a bulldog.''

"So we just keep her breathing until he points some other way," I said.

"If she's innocent," Eliot said. He crossed one leg over the other. "Is it sensible to assume that some gang of drug and sex peddlers would choose to select this lady's pad—pads, for God's sake—on two successive nights to commit murders? I mean, if she doesn't have any connection with them? The first time there might be any number of freak explanations. But the second time, they follow her to where she goes and stage a repeat performance. She's not connected with them? Even with his hunger for headlines Keegan would be a dummy not to follow that lead.''

I didn't say anything because I couldn't think of anything to say. I would have sworn on a stack of Bibles that she wasn't a killer, certainly not last night when I'd been with her for five hours. But connected to the killer or killers in some fashion was something else again.

"I might be some use to you, Mark, if you'll make a trade with me," Eliot said.

"What kind of trade?"

"Give me the inside on what develops here at the Beaumont and I, in return, will give you a hatful of information on the late Jeb McCandless."

"Valerie's father?"

"In person. He died about three years ago—1977. The masterminds who run my news service thought there might be a feature story on old Jeb. He had been a pirate, a power, a hidden force behind governments. He owned a piece of everything worth owning—transportations, communications, oil, coal, steel, pharmaceutical supplies. You name it, he had a piece of it. A big story on Jeb McCandless seemed obvious. I was assigned. I saw your lady just once, at the old man's funeral. She wouldn't talk then, and I never got to try later. Can you guess why?"

"She doesn't like going public," I said.

"Among the things I said Jeb McCandless owned was communications. Would you believe he'd owned a piece of International, my outfit? I wasn't very far into my research when I was called off."

"By Valerie Summers?"

"No, I don't think she had anything to do with the power aspects of his world. There were boards, and trustees, and God knows who else. The name up front was one of his executors, a lawyer named Gardner Fails. Unless I'm mistaken, he owns a piece of your hotel. Or old Jeb owned it and Fails controls that share now."

I stared at Eliot. "Did you know that Gardner Fails brought Valerie Summers here to the Beaumont yesterday, as a place to keep her safe?"

Eliot stared back. Then he punched out his cigarette in the ashtray and lit a fresh one. "He'd be the logical person for her to turn to in trouble," he said.

"So she did. Fails had the power to stop International from doing the McCandless story?"

"Fails represented the power that had that power," Eliot said. "There was never any story in depth about Jeb McCandless, just elaborate obituaries. What was there to hide? I didn't have the assignment any longer, but I've nosed around a bit ever since. There could be a story on why there mustn't be a story, I told myself."

"And is there? Was there?"

"No man with old Jeb's kind of power and influence is ever snow white," Eliot said. "There are always double crosses, and triple crosses, and maneuverings. When such a man dies there are others left who still will profit from those under-the-table dealings. I haven't been able to put my finger on them or I might have a best seller in the works."

"Is Valerie Summers someone who might be profiting from one of those under-the-table deals?" I asked.

"So strangers are murdered in her bedroom?" Eliot brought his open hand down on the arm of his chair. "You may have something there, Mark! Someone is trying to get her to say yes or no about something. She's refused and they're out to scare the hell out of her!"

"By murdering a couple of cheap punks?"

"And planting them on her," Eliot said.

That was too far out, and I told him so. "Maybe you should go to writing that best seller after all," I said. "With that kind of imagination..."

He leaned back in his chair. "Well, it was fun trying," he said. "So let me point out something to you, chum. Any case that can be as crazy as this one is out front can be even crazier when you dig down below the surface. This one makes no sense at all, Mark."

SENSE OR NOT, there were two dead men in the city morgue. Sense or not, bloody violence had invaded the world of the Beaumont. Sense or not, someone was taking dead aim at a harassed Valerie Summers. Maybe I was being naïve to suppose that she had no more idea than the rest of us about what was happening. Maybe she was her father's daughter, raised on what Eliot had called the double and triple crosses of the power world. Either way she was in deep trouble. Someone could be warning her, by leaving dead men as calling cards, that this is what would happen to her if she didn't meet certain demands. Keegan could be right, and she could be a monstrous spider woman, tempting the flies into her web, and leaving them there, dead, for her enemies to see and be warned. Next week, *The War of the Worlds,* I thought. How absurd could you get? Maybe we needed background to explain facts, as Chambrun had suggested, but right now, as far as I was aware, we had no facts to try to explain except two dead men. The music goes round and round and keeps coming out at the same place— nowhere!

When I wasn't certain of my next move—and boy, was I uncertain!—Chambrun had to be my port of call. Should I be on my way out to Ohio to find out what I could about the lives of Mr. and Mrs. Richard Summers? Should I be trying to talk to Valerie again, armed with just a little more than I'd had last night? Should I be hunting down Paul Spector, the Tucson cowboy, and trying to get him to open up with a little more than he'd given us this morning? A trip out into the wilds didn't appeal to me. Somehow I wanted to justify staying close to Valerie, who appeared to need help, and sympathy, and someone to hang onto. It would please me to be that someone.

I wandered down the second floor corridor to Chambrun's office, expecting to find Maggie Madison, the stand-in secretary, in the outer office. Instead, Ruysdale was back on the job, looking fresh as a daisy and twice as pretty.

"The boss has been wondering about you," she said.

"I tried to reach him after I'd seen Derek Newton," I said, "but Maggie told me he was in some kind of meeting with the board of directors."

Ruysdale's smile lacked humor. "They've been telling him how to handle a crisis," she said. "He's not in the best of moods. I think you can go in if you're prepared to be scorched a little."

Well, I may not have done anything right, but I hadn't done anything wrong. I took the chance and went through into the Inner Sanctum.

Chambrun was standing with his back to me, at the windows that look down over the park. He turned, as I was confronted by the hanging judge, eyes as cold as pale marbles.

"It would be a delight," he said, his voice dangerously quiet, "if someone had something sensible to say to me. Would you believe that the board of directors has warned me that murder is not good for the Beaumont's reputation? Idiots!" When I didn't speak he went on. "The unhappy fact is that murder is good for business. Would you believe that we've turned away about three hundred people who decided to have lunch here and listen to the dirt?"

"I don't have much," I said.

"Anything at all is much the way the dice are rolling," he said. He crossed over to his desk and sat down.

"Do you know where Fails and Lukens took Valerie?" I asked him.

"They're in my penthouse on the top of the hotel," he said. "Only place we could think of they'd be sure of privacy. They have to plan some kind of strategy for Mrs. Summers. Keegan is starting to breathe hard. And you, Mark?"

I told him about my visit with Derek Newton. The only contact he'd had with Valerie since her marriage to Dick Summers five years ago had been a telephone call some three months ago after Eleanor Payson's plane had crashed and burned outside of Tucson.

"A person can change dramatically in five years," I said. "As Derek knew her, remembers her, it's unthinkable that she could be directly involved with this kind of violence. But Derek asked the question himself: is she still the same girl he knew before her marriage?"

Chambrun didn't comment. He sat staring down at the yellow legal pad in front of him, scratching meaningless little doodles on it with a ballpoint pen. It was a habit of his whenever he's only half listening. He was, I thought, way up ahead of me on the road, wherever it led.

I told him about my conversation with Eliot Stevens. He gave me a quick, sharp look.

"You promised Stevens a scoop?" he asked.

"Eliot's a friend," I said. "When I've talked to him off the record he's never broken a confidence. Should

I take him up on his offer and go through the stuff he has on Jeb McCandless?''

Chambrun pushed aside his pad and put down the pen. ''Gardner Fails is the executor of Jeb Mc-Candless's personal estate,'' he said. ''There were probably dozens of scandals in the old man's life, business and personal. He was married four times. His first three wives may be floating around somewhere. It would be Fails' quite proper desire to let his client rest in peace. If he had the leverage to keep International from running a lurid feature on the old man, he was right to use it.''

''But if something from the old man's past is behind what's happening to Valerie?''

''She was left money, not control of her father's business holdings,'' Chambrun said.

''She could be trying to keep something about her father from being revealed,'' I said.

Chambrun sounded impatient. ''By shooting a couple of street punks in the head?''

''So you've moved over to my side of the street,'' I said. ''You don't believe she can be guilty of killing?''

''There's nothing to take hold of yet to believe,'' he said. ''My one concern at the moment is to make certain that whatever is going on be stopped now, dead in its tracks. If the lady is guilty, she must be stopped. If someone is out to destroy her, they must be stopped.''

''You think there's more to come?''

''I would bet on it,'' he said.

And, as usual, he was right. The door to the office opened and Jerry Dodd came in. Betsy Ruysdale was just behind him, standing in the doorway. Looking at

their faces I didn't have to be told that there was
something new.

"Strike three!" Jerry said, his voice harsh.

Chambrun was instantly standing. "Are you saying—?"

"Once more," Jerry said. "We came down from
your penthouse, the lady, Fails, Andy Lukens, one of
my men and one of Keegan's cops. The lady was covered like a tent from the moment she woke up. When
we got back to the twelfth floor the man who was
supposed to be stationed in the hall there was missing. We supposed he'd gone for a quick cup of coffee, or to the john, or something. We used Mrs.
Summers' key to open the door of 1216 and the cop
and I went in with her. There it was. The same scene—
the same goddamn scene. Man with a hole in his head
lying on the floor beside the bed."

Chambrun muttered something under his breath.

"There's one slight difference in the scenario,"
Jerry said. "This time we knew immediately who the
dead man was. Sergeant Polansky, the missing cop."

"My God, I just talked to him about an hour ago,"
I said.

"That will entitle you to a box seat at the party,"
Jerry said. "The whole damned police force is going
to be down on our heads. They don't like cop killers."

PART TWO

ONE

ANY CHANCE IN THE WORLD that this wouldn't make every headline and every television screen in the country was gone from the start. The lobby was already crowded with reporters when the police began to pour in. There was no possibility of hiding from them that a police sergeant had been murdered, and like the two killings before that, in Valerie Summers' living quarters.

Once more Valerie was swept away from where she was supposed to be living. This time Keegan had commandeered one of the conference rooms on the lobby level as a headquarters for himself. Just as I got to the lobby myself Valerie was herded through the crowd of reporters and gaping guests by a squad of cops. It required physical force to get her past them all and into the conference room. Andy Lukens was with her, I was grateful for that. I don't know if she saw me or not. She was being literally held up and dragged along by Keegan's men. Cameras flashed and I could hear the steady whir of a television camera, located on the mezzanine balcony, I thought.

I fought off the press people and followed after Valerie. I didn't have anything to tell anyone—except Keegan. He wasn't with the cops surrounding Valerie and I wasn't allowed into the conference room. A cop barring the door told me Keegan was still up on the twelfth floor.

Elevators were crowded with reporters and curious people trying to get to where it was at. I went around to the rear of the lobby and took the service elevator up to twelve. The curious hadn't thought of that access yet.

Twelve was a madhouse, the corridor crammed with people. Two uniformed cops were blocking the door to 1216. They told me to go peddle my papers. Just then Keegan stepped out from the room. I could see his crew at work through the open door. Keegan's face was a dark thundercloud.

"I don't need your help, Haskell," he said to me.

"I've got something for you that may be helpful," I said.

"Like what?"

"I was up here about noon. I had a conversation with Polansky."

He reached out, took me by the arm with what felt like an iron claw, and almost dragged me back into the room. Polansky, God help me, was still there, the side of his head blown open. I thought for a minute I was going to throw up.

"I came up here just about twelve o'clock," I told Keegan, "to see whether I could talk to Mrs. Summers. I hadn't called on the phone in case she was still asleep. Polansky was out there in the hall. The maid was in here making up the room."

"What maid?"

"I don't know. Whoever's assigned to this floor."

"You talked to Joe?"

"If that's Polansky's name, yes. He told me Mrs. Summers had gone somewhere with her lawyers, along with some of the men assigned to guard her."

"Chambrun's penthouse. I gave them permission," Keegan said.

"So she's in the clear," I said. "He was fine when I saw him at twelve o'clock. She was in the penthouse."

"She didn't pull the trigger," Keegan said. "How much in the clear she is we'll find out. Get that maid for me."

The maid was in the housekeeper's room down the hall in a panic. I took her back to 1216 and the cops let us in. She screamed when she saw the medical examiner's man bent over the body. Her story was straightforward enough. The housekeeper had gotten a call from Betsy Ruysdale saying that now would be a good time to make up the room. She'd gone down the hall with her cleaning wagon, been questioned by Polansky, allowed to go in. That was all. She'd done her job and left. Polansky had been at his post when she went back to her quarters.

"How thoroughly did you go over the room?" Keegan asked.

"It's a regular routine," the maid said, keeping her eyes turned away from the bloodied corpse.

"You look in the closet, the bathroom?"

"There's a laundry hamper in the closet," the maid said. "We always look there to see if there are any linens to take out. I cleaned the bathroom, put in fresh towels."

"Nobody could have been hiding in there?"

"Oh my, no!" the maid said. "There's just this room, the bathroom, the closet."

"Under the bed?" Keegan suggested.

"I ran the vacuum under it from both sides," she said.

Keegan told her a cop would take a statement from her in a while, not to go anywhere till that happened. She hurried off, almost running.

"Same goes for you," Keegan said to me. "I'll want your conversation with Polansky, every damn word of it. Don't get lost."

A plainclothes cop who had been searching the bureau drawers while we talked called out to Keegan. "Surprise, Lieutenant!" he said.

Keegan had to walk around the body and the medical examiner's man who was bent over it to get to the bureau.

"Right in among her underclothes," the plainclothes cop said.

Keegan looked, and I heard him mutter something under his breath. He took a ballpoint pen out of his pocket and fished into the drawer with it. He brought it out, poked through the trigger guard of a small pearl-handled gun.

"Maybe we've struck oil at last," Keegan said. "It's the right caliber." He held it up so that he could sniff at the barrel. "Recently fired." He turned to the plainclothes man. "Lift any fingerprints, Dawson, and then rush it down to Ballistics. We can have the little lady wrapped up if it checks out." He passed over the gun, still held by the pen, to Dawson, and turned to the medical examiner's man. "You make a guess as to when, Mac?"

The medical technician stood up, wiping his hands on a handkerchief. "You know we can't be too accurate till we get the body down to the morgue, Lieutenant. Anywhere from a little less than an hour to not more than two hours is my guess.''

I glanced at my watch. It was going on two o'clock. The body had been found by Jerry Dodd almost an hour ago. It had taken that much time for Keegan and his crew to assemble and go through the preliminaries.

''He was alive at twelve o'clock,'' I said. ''I talked to him out there in the hall just a few minutes after twelve. The lady was up in the penthouse then with her lawyers, watched over by two of Jerry Dodd's men and one of yours, Lieutenant. She came back here with Jerry, his men, your man, and they found the body. No way on earth she could have been involved.''

''You like to explain the gun?'' Keegan asked. ''I'll bet you a month's pay it will turn out to be the weapon used to murder three men.''

''But not by Valerie Summers this third time,'' I said. ''No way.''

''Maybe she's had a partner all along,'' Keegan said.

This Black Irishman wasn't a man to let go once he had his teeth sunk into a victim's throat. I found myself thinking of a remark of Mark Twain's to the effect that ''. . . it's a wonderful sight to watch the calm and confidence of a Christian—who holds four aces!'' I thought that pearl-handled gun looked like a fourth ace to Keegan.

I HAD AN ADVANTAGE over Keegan's army relating to the territory. I know every back corridor and hallway and rear door in the Beaumont. The conference room

where Valerie was being held is entered by the public
from a door in the lobby. But, like most public rooms,
there is a rear way in used by waiters for serving food,
drinks, and other needs of the people using the place.
We don't let waiters with trays or food wagons make
a traffic stream through the lobby. That particular
conference facility is called the Carnation Room.
Keegan's cops were barring the lobby door to the press
and to a small army of the curious who were waiting
and hoping for something to happen.

I went down from 1216 to the service area and the
rear door of the Carnation. I was delighted to find no
one standing guard there and I let myself in. There was
a long table surrounded by chairs for the board of directors. Valerie and Andy Lukens were the only people in the room. She was sitting at the table, head bent
forward, face buried in her hands. Andy Lukens, her
lawyer, was walking restlessly up and down, chewing
on the stem of his unlighted pipe.

"Mark!" he said. "They let you in?"

"Magic trick," I said. "Keegan doesn't know about
the back door—yet." Valerie lowered her hands, and
those violet eyes were dark with shock and relief.
"They found your gun," I said.

The eyes went blank. "What are you talking about,
Mark? I don't own a gun!"

"Pearl-handled, the right caliber. It's on the way to
Ballistics. I would guess the chances are good it will
turn out to be the weapon used to kill three men. If it
does, your troubles are going to multiply, Val."

She brought a clenched fist down on the table. *"I
don't own a gun! I've never owned a gun!"*

"It was in your bureau drawer, amongst your undies, according to the cop."

"Fingerprints?" Andy asked.

"Being checked."

"They won't find mine," Valerie said. "I don't own a gun and I've never handled a gun—not ever!"

"It's more of the same," Andy said. "Elaborate frame-up."

"Who and why?" I said.

"My God, Mark, I've said it over and over again," Valerie said. "There's no one I know of who would want to hurt me. It's completely meaningless to me, completely senseless."

"It's happened. It's happening," I said.

The rear door to the Carnation Room opened and there was Chambrun, looking dapper in a gray, tropical-worsted summer suit.

"One of Jerry's men saw you make it the back way, Mark. I thought I'd try it, too," he said.

He sat down on the edge of the table while I brought him up-to-date, his eyes fixed the whole time on Valerie. She looked like someone in a trance.

"Mark's right," Chambrun said, when I'd finished. "The gun will turn out to be the murder weapon. There's no other reason to plant it on Mrs. Summers."

"But it won't hold up in the killing of Polansky," I said. "He was alive after Valerie had gone up to your penthouse. She was under observation every second until he was found."

"You say Keegan suggests a 'partner in crime'?"

"Anything to fit his theory," I said.

Chambrun tapped one of his flat, Egyptian cigarettes on the back of his silver case. "There are some interesting variations in this Polansky case, differences from the other two," he said. He slipped the case back in his pocket and lit the cigarette with his Dunhill lighter. His eyes were narrowed against the smoke. "Carl Rogers and Willie Bloomfield were out of the same jungle—drugs, sex, pornography. Polansky was a cop with a good record. I've checked. Rogers and Bloomfield had been dead about four hours when they were found. Polansky, thanks to the fact that you saw him at noon, Mark, can't have been dead for more than an hour when he was found, probably less. Mrs. Summers *could* have been responsible for the first two. There's no way in the world she can have been responsible for Polansky."

"Except as an accessory," Andy Lukens said.

"Mr. Lukens, if you think I—" Valerie began.

"Devil's advocate," he said, smiling at her. "I'm trying to think like Keegan so I'll be ready for him."

"So what do we have?" Chambrun asked. "Polansky is alive and well at noon, standing guard out in the hall. Not too long after that the wheels begin to turn. The maid was there when you saw him, Mark. He let her in."

"She'd have her own key," Andy said.

"He permitted her to go in," Chambrun said. "She finished her job, left, and he was at his post. Now we come to fun and games. There's no back way into that single room like Five A, the suite where Willie Bloomfield got his. There was no way into that room except by going past Polansky."

"So he left his post," Andy Lukens said.

"Possibly not, but I think not in the sense you mean," Chambrun said. "This is a well-trained, responsible policeman. He's up to his eyebrows in a complex murder case. He's supposed to guard a room, he'll guard it. So, he suddenly feels sick? He sees something he thinks he should report to Keegan? I don't think he strolls away somewhere to find a phone or a public bathroom. I think he goes *into* the room to find the phone—or the plumbing. He's still guarding the room that way. That's what a trained cop would do, I think."

"But he leaves the hall door open, the killer goes in after him, kills him, plants the gun in Val's bureau, and walks away," Andy Lukens suggested.

Chambrun stared at the end of his cigarette, scowling. He cupped his left hand and let the ash drop into it. "It could be that way," he said. "It would be careless of Polansky to leave the hall door open, even unlocked. But it could be that way." He slipped down off the table and walked beside the polished surface to an ashtray. He emptied the ash from his hand. His back was to us for a moment, and then he turned. "What happens, Andrew, if the gun turns out to be the weapon used in all three murders?"

Andy Lukens shrugged. "Keegan will have himself a problem," he said. "He can't prove the gun belongs to Val, because it doesn't. She's absolutely clear in the shooting of Polansky. The only thing he's possibly got is 'accessory to murder.' He can't hold her in jail on that. I'd have her out in half an hour."

"Maybe it would be better if he could hold her," Chambrun said.

"Mr Chambrun—" Val began.

"My dear Mrs. Summers," Chambrun said, "I have the feeling you're in the gravest kind of danger. Someone is taking dead aim at you. How do we keep you safe?"

"I'd say the Beaumont was as safe as any place she could find," Andy said.

Chambrun's smile had a bitter twist to it. "That would be a rib-splitting joke if you said it in public. Two men murdered in less than twenty-four hours; the killer, his identity not even guessed at, probably standing on the other side of that door and watching Keegan's whole charade, laughing up his sleeve. Worse than that, *he's not finished*. If the gun doesn't do Mrs. Summers in, he'll have to make another try."

Valerie's voice was unsteady. "I—I'd like to just walk away, hide out there, somewhere where people don't know who I am or care who I am."

"You were hiding in your apartment on Tenth Street and you were found," Chambrun said. "The danger you're facing is complicated if you're telling us the truth, Mrs. Summers. The person who's out to harm you found you on Tenth Street. It was no problem for him to follow you here. It will be no problem for him if you 'just walk away.' You don't know who to hide from, we don't know who to stop. He holds all the cards—unless you can put us on the track."

"I keep telling you—!"

"I know what you keep telling us Mrs. Summers. You have no enemies—but you *do*. There is no one who wants to punish you for something—but there *is*!"

"Oh my God," Valerie said, turning her head from side to side. She was very close to cracking up completely, I thought.

"We're dealing with a sick mind, Valerie," Chambrun said. "You're looking for some enormous encounter, some vivid clash with someone. You can't think of any so you say you have no enemy, you have not consciously hurt anybody, crossed anybody. You're certain no one has a motive."

"Money," Andy Lukens said.

"I don't think so," Chambrun said. "If Valerie is telling us the truth."

"You keep saying that!" she cried out. " 'If' I'm telling you the truth. I am! I have been!"

"No one has tried to blackmail you, get money from you under pressure of some sort?"

"No, no, no!"

Chambrun punched out his cigarette in the ashtray on the long table and walked down the room to stand by Valerie's chair. His voice was gentle, compassionate.

"You're a lovely woman, Valerie," he said. "Men must have been after you all your life. It would be unnatural if they haven't been. You must have had the same choice to make, over and over; to say yes or no. Saying no must have been almost a routine. I can imagine your being kind about it. You were flattered but no thank you. I'll bet you can't count the number of noes. Somewhere along the way—not yesterday, maybe months ago, maybe years ago—you may have said no to someone whose sick pride couldn't take the rejection. You thought it was routine and you've forgotten about it. It was an everyday thing. But that sick mind has let his anger cook and cook until it has boiled over.''

"There's no such person!" Valerie said.

"You don't know if there is or not," Chambrun said. "You haven't been inside that sick mind. I'm just trying to make you see that this sick mind can have made a motive out of something that you don't even remember. So let's forget a rejected lover for a moment. I understood that over the years you have given money for medical research, to the arts in one form or another. You must have been asked for help many times when you had to say no. You had to use judgment, you had to choose who you would help. If you said yes to everyone you'd soon have been poverty stricken. So, routinely, you said no to someone with a sick mind, and his resentment has cooked and cooked—and he has chosen now for a payoff. We have to dig back in your past, Valerie, for something you haven't remembered yet as any kind of crisis.''

Her eyes were wide. "You're talking about psycho-analysis," she said.

"I'm afraid we don't have time for that technique," he said. "Just talking to a friend, going through the memory book of your mind. You'll find what you're looking for yourself, if you'll take the time to talk and remember.''

"I don't have any friends."

"Mark is your friend, I am your friend."

"I am your friend," Andy Lukens said.

"You, Andrew, are her lawyer," Chambrun said. "Keegan and the district attorney are your business.''

As if it was a stage cue the lobby door was opened. A thunder of voices swept in, reporters shouting questions. Keegan came in, followed by a young man carrying a leather briefcase. The door was shut and the voices silenced.

"How did you two characters get in here?" Keegan demanded. He was talking to Chambrun and me.

Chambrun gestured toward the rear door. "No one stopped us so we came," he said.

"Sonofabitch!" Keegan said. Then he turned to the man with the briefcase. "This is Tom Oldham, Assistant D.A."

Oldham, sandy-haired, sharp-eyed, nodded to us. Keegan turned back to the lobby door, opened it, and called out, "Moran!" The voices inundated us again as a uniformed cop came in. "We overlooked a rear entrance," Keegan said. "Get someone there."

Moran went to the rear door, taking the post himself. Keegan turned to Valerie. "So Haskell has had time to tell you what we found upstairs."

She didn't answer.

"As I suspected, the gun we found in your bureau drawer was used in all three killings," Keegan said. "Ballistics says there's no question."

"But it's not her gun," Andy Lukens said.

"So she says—naturally," Keegan said.

"And she didn't kill Polansky," I said.

Keegan was shaking with anger. "You two characters get out of here!" he shouted at us. "We have police business with the lady!"

Valerie reached out a hand to Chambrun. He took it, held it for a moment. "Just tell the lieutenant what you can," he said. "We'll be standing by."

We walked past Moran and out into the service area.

"When he's through with her," Chambrun said to me, "I'm going to put her up in my penthouse. It's the least accessible place in the hotel. Then you're going to talk to her till she's dumb with fatigue. What we need to know is buried there, somewhere."

Chambrun had finally got something eating at me. We weren't just trying to solve a problem. There was a killer, nutty as a fruitcake, deadly as a cobra, circulating in our world, and he was watching us! Get in his way as Polansky had done and we could expect violence just as swift and just as deadly. He could be on the next bar stool to me, in the same elevator, circulating in the same public rooms, and there wasn't the remotest clue to who he was or what he looked like. If I started fishing into Valerie's past for an explanation to all this, I could very well find myself becoming a target for this creep. Not a very appetizing thought, or one designed to keep you from looking back over your shoulder.

Chambrun left me in the service area, taking his private elevator to the roof, presumably to make arrangements for moving Valerie into his penthouse. I went up a flight of stairs to the balcony that circles the lobby at the mezzanine level.

The lobby looked like the outside of a bank that has failed, with a couple hundred depositors waiting outside of the locked door hoping to get their money out. The locked door was the door to the Carnation Room. On the other side of it was a rich and beautiful lady who might, the rumor was, have killed three men in cold blood. That was money in the bank as far as their avid curiosity was concerned. Sooner or later she would have to come out, and they could reach out to touch her, shout questions at her, take pictures of her, destroy any chance she had for privacy in the next ten years. Someone, I thought, should be giving orders to keep people moving, but the men and women representing newspapers, radio stations, television networks, and scandal magazines wouldn't move unless the police brought in a riot squad and drove them out. I realized that they represented two-thirds of the crowd waiting outside the Carnation Room. I knew most of them by sight, had had dealings with all of them at one time or another over the years. Most of the others were hotel guests and regular patrons of our bars and restaurants. I realized there weren't more than ten or twelve people, four or five of them women, who were total strangers to me. Unfortunately the killer wouldn't have a bright star in the middle of his forehead to help me pick him out. Looking at those few strange faces I had an idea that hadn't struck me before. Except for Keegan and his fixation on Valerie, the rest of us had been thinking of the killer as a man. Why not a woman? That little pearl-handled gun was a woman's weapon. A woman could be nursing a psychotic grudge against Val just as readily as a man. The wife or girlfriend of a man who had left her for Val? In the arts, an actress, singer, dancer, writer, sculptor, asking for help and being turned down? Val might not have known such an applicant personally. In none of the three deaths had there been any sign of physical struggle or encounter of any sort. Each time it appeared the victim had been caught totally by surprise, gunned down before he could lift a finger to protect himself. In Polansky's case that was hard to accept. He had been a trained officer; he had been armed and on guard against any kind of trouble. He'd apparently never reached for his gun, obviously never gotten it out of its holster. A woman might explain how he'd been caught so flatfooted, unprepared.

I thought, sourly, that Gloria Steinem would applaud me for giving women their equal rights in my thinking. I leaned forward, elbows on the balcony rail, studying those dozen unfamiliar faces in the crowd outside the door of the Carnation Room. I wanted to be sure to remember if one of them turned up in this same frame of reference again. You don't wander into the Beaumont's lobby wearing blue jeans and a T-shirt. Those strangers all looked as though they belonged; conservative but not inexpensive.

A heavy hand suddenly rested on my shoulder. I jumped a foot and spun around. I wasn't going to be happy for some time about the unexpected. I found myself facing a scowling Tucson cowboy. I wondered if I was about to find myself looking down the barrel of Paul Spector's six-shooter—if he carried one. That's how jumpy I was.

"What the hell's goin' on down there?" he demanded.

"You know there's been another killing?" I asked him.

"Just heard it on the radio in my hotel room. Cop! I came on the run. Is it the one who was out to get Val?"

"One of his men. They found a gun in Val's room that turns out to have killed all three."

"Oh, Jesus!" Spector said.

"But Val couldn't have killed the cop," I said. "She's alibied for every second of the time when it could have happened."

He took a deep breath and let it out in a sign of relief. "She in that room down there?"

I nodded.

"No one helpin' her?"

"She's got a lawyer."

"Fails?" He spoke the name as though the idea outraged him.

"Chambrun got her a good criminal lawyer," I said. "You sound like you don't like Gardner Fails."

"Damned ol' goat!" he said. "Would you believe he used to come visit Jeb in Tucson. Val was floating around, ten, eleven years old. Beautiful kid. That ol' jerk would take every chance he had to give her behind a lovin' pinch! I can hear him now." Spector gave an absurd imitation. "'Come sit in Uncle Gardner's lap, honey.' And then he'd pinch her bosoms which were just startin' to grow."

"And when she got to be a woman?"

"Oh, hell, I guess all men feel kinda hungry when they look at Val. How about you, Haskell? Don't you feel anything?"

I tried smiling at him. "*Hungry* may be the word," I said.

"You an' that fancy boss of yours really tryin' to help her?" he asked.

"Really. All the way," I said.

"I feel so damn helpless!" he said. "I'd like to go in and punch that Keegan right in the nose! Doesn't he know he's got hold of the wrong end of this thing?"

"Process of elimination. He'll find out," I said.

"How long's he goin' to keep her in there?"

"He's got an assistant D.A. with him. It could be minutes or hours."

"An' then what?"

"Chambrun will hide Val away somewhere and try to point Keegan in the right direction."

"Why hide her away? Why does she have to hide?"

"Keegan isn't the enemy," I said. "He's just a stubborn cop turning everything that comes his way over and over. Someone else we haven't even guessed at is the enemy." I tried my newest notion out on him for size. "You know any woman who may hate Val?"

He laughed, not with humor. "Women can't stand women they can't compete with," he said. "For my dough there ain't a woman in the world who can compete with Val, so there must be dozens of 'em who hate her guts. Why?"

"I've started to smell a woman in this case," I said.

"There's a big gap in time for me," Spector said.

"Meaning?"

"Four years in college, when I just saw her a couple of summers; six years after that, five of marriage and almost a whole year since Dick Summers got his, when I didn't see her except for the few days she spent in Tucson for ol' Jeb's funeral."

There was something wrong about those figures I thought. Val had been advertised to us by Fails as being thirty years old. What Spector was telling me was that she'd been twenty before she went to Vassar. That was late for an obviously bright girl. She had been past twenty, then, when she'd proposed a love affair to Derek Newton, at the same time admitting gravely that it would be a "first" for her if the idea pleased him.

"From the time she was three till the time she was twenty I saw her almost every day of her life," Spector was saying. "After that, hardly ever. It wasn't till she went away to Vassar that she had a chance to make enemies."

"How come?" I asked.

"You can't imagine what it was like down there in Tucson," Spector said. "For her, I mean. Hundreds of acres of land, a house like a palace, cottages for the help, horses, cars, cattle. But it was like an iron fence was built around the property—although there wasn't any fence. The hands, like me, were really a police force. No stranger could wander into the property without being stopped, questioned, given the third degree. Val was never allowed to leave the grounds without someone with her. She never went to school like an ordinary kid. There was a succession of tutors and teachers. Oh, there were parties, and a lot of high ol' times, but always inside that fence that wasn't there."

"Why?"

"Bee in the ol' man's bonnet," Spector said. "I guess he'd walked over and stepped on a thousand people in his time. That's how you get to be his kind of rich. The way he saw it there was just one way he could be had, one way someone could get back at him. Someone would kidnap Val, demand a huge ransom, maybe hurt, or destroy, or disfigure the one person he loved. So he never let her out of his sight or the sight of someone he trusted. She wanted to go to a movie, he got the film for her and she saw it in a projection room he had in the house. She wanted kids to play with, they had to come to her, and they were watched over every second, their parents were watched over. He had two strong-arm boys who were his private body-guards and sort of personal detectives. They'd work up a file on everybody who came to the spread. I'll bet there are records on a thousand people they investigated over the years, locked away somewhere."

"Some childhood!"

"Oh, she had everything," Spector said. "Her own riding horses, her own cars, clothes for a princess. But she couldn't go outside that fence without an army with her."

"That fence that didn't exist."

"Oh, it existed for her. It existed just as though it was twenty feet high. I remember one day when she was about fourteen she got past the fence one day, riding on her cow pony. Ten minutes later the ol' man's private helicopter landed beside her and she was dragged home like an escaped prisoner. She was watched over every minute of every day and every night."

"But he finally let her go to college; late, but let her go," I said.

Spector frowned down at the mob outside the door of the Carnation Room. The woman he was "hungry" for was on the other side of that door with Keegan doing God knows what to her. "She tried to kill herself," he said.

I was jolted.

"A hot bath, a razor blade, slashed wrists, a note saying she was sorry. She didn't even have the privacy to die. There wasn't any lock on the bathroom door.

A personal maid, whose job it was to look out for her, found her in time." Spector looked at me. "You can still see the scars on her wrists if she's wearing a short-sleeved dress."

"That shook up Jeb McCandless?"

"Damn near killed him," Spector said. "It couldn't be kept a secret. Doctors, ambulances, everyone on the spread knew about it. When she came back from the hospital ol' Jeb threw in the towel. He saw that she had to have a life of her own, freedom, or going on living was worthless to her. All the clothes, and the horses, and the cars weren't worth a damn to her. He had to let her have her way or he'd lose her forever. I got to hand it to him. The danger he was afraid of was still there, but if he cared a damn for her he had to risk it."

"So she changed her name and went out into the world," I said.

"That was the one thing he pleaded for. She couldn't call herself McCandless. That name could attract danger like a magnet. I drove them to the airport that day she took off for the East. She was bubbling over with excitement like a bottle of freshly opened champagne. He was eighty-six years old that fall day. He watched that plane take off into the sky and he cried like a baby." Spector shook his head as if to rid himself of that memory. "It's no fun to watch a strong man bawl," he said. "But things worked out better than he dreamed they would. She did fine in college, good marks, good reports. She was a different person when she came home for the first summer vacation. Back in Tucson she had to stay inside the 'fence,' but it didn't matter anymore. She knew she

could take off tomorrow. She and the ol' man were
very close that first summer. It was her way of thank-
ing him, to be close to him. There was this professor
she had a crush on, but that evidently didn't work. She
talked about him a lot, dreamed about him, I guess.
But when she went back in the fall she wrote to Jeb
and told him it was all off. Then Dick Summers came
on the scene. Here it was, the ol' man thought, someone out to get her money. She brought him out that
third summer, and he turned out to be an honest-to-
God man. I could see ol' Jeb relax for the first time in
a long time. She'd found a future for herself that had
nothing to do with the dangers of being a Mc-
Candless. Thank God he didn't live to see Dick die, or
this present hell. In a way I wish he had. He had the
money, the strength, the power to push that crazy
Keegan right off the stage!''

At that moment the door to the Carnation Room
opened and Keegan and Oldham, the Assistant D.A.,
appeared. Val and Lukens were not with them. Keegan was fighting off the reporters, shouting at them
that he had nothing new to tell them. At least he'd
saved Val that encounter.

"Where is she?'' Spector asked me.

"There's another way out. She's got her lawyer with
her, and Keegan has a man inside who could be with
her.''

"I'm gonna find her,'' Spector said.

I stopped him as he started to move away. "Take a
look at those people down there,'' I said. "You see
anyone down there who could belong to Valerie's
Tucson world? Or the McCandless business world?''

Spector gave it an honest try, I thought, searching for someone in a crew of a couple hundred people who might ring a bell for him. Suddenly he stretched out his arm and pointed. "That tall, sandy-haired guy with the glasses," he said. "He's a reporter for some newspaper syndicate. Covered ol' Jeb's funeral in Tucson back in '77. He's the only one I recall seein' before."

He was indicating my friend Eliot Stevens, International's man. Not a likely suspect.

"Let's find her," Spector said.

We went down the fire stairs to the service area and in the back door of the Carnation Room. Moran wasn't on guard anymore. The room was empty.

We went up to the second floor and down the hall to Chambrun's office. Maggie Madison was filling in for Betsy Ruysdale again in the outer office.

"They've all gone up to the roof," she said. "I was told to tell you to report there if I saw you, Mr. Haskell."

Spector turned to follow me.

"I can't take you up there without getting permission," I told him. "You stay here with Maggie, and if they'll let you see her, I'll call you."

"Anybody tries to stop me seein' her," Spector said, "and I may jes' start takin' this stinkin' place apart, brick by brick!"

There are three penthouses on the roof of the Beaumont. One of them is Chambrun's, one of them is leased by the United Nations and is kept for special diplomatic and political dignitaries from all over the world, the third was long ago bought as a co-op by a marvelous, impossible, eccentric, charming lady who

has lived there for the last thirty years with a series of
mean-tempered little black-and-white Japanese span-
iels. Dogs are against the rules in the Beaumont, but
there are no rules made by man that Victoria Haven
will obey if they displeased her. More about this extraordinary octogenarian later on.

Chambrun had referred to his penthouse as "the
least accessible" place in the hotel. That went for all
three penthouses. The main banks of elevators go only
to the fortieth floor. There is only one that goes to the
roof and it is, in effect, for the private use of Chambrun, Mrs. Haven, and the United Nations. It isn't
available to the general public and you can't get a ride
in it unless the operator knows you have legitimate
business with one of the rooftop tenants. I'm a privi-
leged character with a permanent pass which I seldom
use.

One of Jerry Dodd's men was operating that car
and he took me up to the roof. Chambrun's penthouse is his area of total privacy. In all the years I've
worked for him I don't think I've been in it more than
a dozen times. In those times, believe it or not, I've
never seen the rear facilities, where, I understand,
there is a small exercise gym, a sauna bath, several
bedrooms, one of which some people believe is re-
served for Betsy Ruysdale. Up front there is a living
room, a library, a kitchen into which I've penetrated
for ice cubes, a lavatory for guests, and French doors
in the living room which open out onto an elegant roof
garden. The living room is something. An oriental rug
that would be hard to look away from if it weren't for
paintings by Matisse, Chagall, and Picasso. There is
what I believe the Steinway people call a "parlor

grand." One of the things most people don't know about Chambrun is that he is a brilliant pianist. That could have been his career if dealing with people hadn't obsessed him.

Moran, Keegan's man, was in the vestibule when I went to the door of Chambrun's penthouse. He gave me a wry smile and a traffic cop's signal to proceed. I went through into the living room. Chambrun and Andy Lukens were there, sipping coffee from china mugs. That suggested that Ruysdale was somewhere. Chambrun won't even boil water for himself.

"The Tucson cowboy is down in your office," I told Chambrun, "threatening to do a Samson on the hotel if he can't see Val."

"Might be a break for her to see someone from home," Andy Lukens said.

Chambrun nodded. "Tell him to come up, Mark."

I went to the phone in the corner and told Maggie Madison to send Spector up, and then to the vestibule to alert Moran that a guest was expected.

"If Spector doesn't pull down the building the press is likely to," I said, when I rejoined Chambrun and Andy. "Is there something we can tell them to keep them quiet?"

"The lady will see nobody," Chambrun said. "You may be the best person to quiet them down, Andrew."

"You might tell me what the quieting words are," he said, "just in case I get snowed under."

"Someone was in the act of planting the murder weapon in Valerie's room when he was interrupted by Polansky, who was shot to death with it," Andy said. "Valerie is totally clear of that murder. No way in the world Keegan can get around that, which makes his whole case a little shaky. No other leads, though. Keegan's questioning maids, elevator operators, bell-boys, other guests on the twelfth floor. Somebody must have seen somebody, he thinks. The twelfth floor was a hot spot once Valerie was moved there. People might have seen things they wouldn't have noticed under normal conditions.''

"You won't get rich betting on it," Chambrun said. He seemed far away, lost in some thinking of his own, yet hearing us.

At that moment Valerie and Betsy Ruysdale came out of the bedroom wing of the penthouse. Ruysdale was her usual, blooming self, but Valerie looked like someone in a trance. The violet eyes looked at me as if I were a stranger. She seemed to need guidance, as though she didn't know where she was. Ruysdale steered her to a chair, suggested coffee which drew a blank, and went off into the kitchen to get it anyway.

"There's a friend of yours on his way up here to see you, Val," Andy said.

"Friend?" she sounded puzzled.

"Paul Spector. I believe he manages your father's property in Tucson."

"Paul here, in New York?"

"He arrived here in the middle of the night," I said. "There's been no chance to get him to you until now. He wants to help if there's some way he can. He's talked a lot about you. He seems very fond of you."

She turned her head from side to side as if she was trying to make it make sense. "I've known him all my life," she said.

"Maybe he can help you remember things that are still elusive," Chambrun said.

"There is nothing to remember!" she said.

Chambrun eyed her steadily. "Where were you a week ago Thursday at two o'clock in the afternoon?" he asked.

"I don't understand," she said. "A week ago Thursday?"

"You were somewhere at two o'clock in the afternoon."

"I...I just don't understand," she said. "Two o'clock a week ago Thursday..."

"Don't struggle with it," Chambrun said. "I'm just trying to make a point, Valerie. You were somewhere at two o'clock a week ago Thursday. If it was important you could eventually dig it out, by going over your routines, your daily doings. That's what we have to do with your past. Just as blank in your memory at the moment as a week ago Thursday is a name, a face, an action, an event which, when we uncover it, may be vital to your future, your safety. It's there. We've got to try to bring it up front."

She gave him a tiny little smile of triumph. "At two o'clock in the afternoon a week ago Thursday I was in a movie theater on Eighth Street watching *Kramer vs. Kramer*," she said.

"Good girl," Chambrun said. "You see, when we try working at it, it may not be so hard after all."

At that point the great Southwest burst into the room. Spector stood just inside the door, took off his Stetson and tossed it in a chair.

"Baby!" he said. "You look great, kid!"

He seemed to be waiting for a cue of some sort, and when he didn't get one he charged across the room, took Val by both arms and lifted her right off the floor. Then he put her down and engulfed her in a bear hug.

"Don't you worry about anythin', baby," he said. "We'll show these crazy cops which end is up." Still holding her by the shoulders he looked around at the people he didn't know. I introduced him to Betsy Ruysdale and Andy Lukens.

"You her lawyer, boy?" Spector asked Andy. "How big is her trouble?"

"Legally, I don't think she has much to worry about," Andy said.

"I tried to explain to you this morning, Mr. Spector," Chambrun said. "Someone has tried to frame Mrs. Summers. The danger now is a direct attack on her."

"I'm stayin' right here," Spector said. "Nobody's goin' to get to her. Not by me!"

"Nobody's going to get to her, with or without you, Mr. Spector," Chambrun said, not impressed. "Our job is to find out who will be trying. Because, whoever he is, he's mad as a hatter, and he will try."

TWO

IT SEEMED LOGICAL to give Valerie some time with her long-time friend, the Tucson cowboy. She had spent the best part of two days and nights being grilled and questioned by Keegan and company. I did think she looked a little startled when the rest of us began a general exit.

"The hotel still has to operate, Valerie," Chambrun said to her. "Ruysdale and I have a lot to catch up on, Mark has an army of press people to be concerned about and Andrew's going to try to stave them off for a while. Be sure that no one can get up here to the roof without my permission, or Keegan's."

"The cops had damn well better let her alone for a while," Spector said. "She's had enough of their insanity."

"There'll be a guard in the outer vestibule and one of my trusted people on the elevator," Chambrun said.

"You've had an army around her twice and it didn't stop this creep!" Spector said.

He was, unfortunately, right.

Chambrun went to the French doors and, beckoning me to follow, walked out into his garden.

"I want to let Mrs. Haven know what's going on up here," he said when I joined him. "Her comings and goings may be a little bit restricted, with police and security people patrolling the place all night."

"The U.N. penthouse unoccupied?" I asked.

"Yes, and we'll keep it that way as long as Valerie is holed in up here. I don't want any strangers anywhere near her."

"You really think she's in danger?"

"If you don't, Mark, you're an idiot," he said. "The problem is to find out from which direction the wind is blowing."

We walked out of his garden and across the roof to Mrs. Haven's penthouse. Chambrun reached out to press the doorbell, but before he touched it the door opened and we were confronted by the lady. She'd obviously seen us coming.

"Well, Pierre, I thought you were going to leave me hanging by my fingernails," she said. She smiled at me, a naughty smile. "Is the lady as pretty as she looks from a distance, Haskell? Is it true, by the way, that gentlemen prefer blondes?"

Victoria Haven is something to look at. At eighty she is tall, ramrod straight. Her hair, quantities of it, is worn piled on top of her head, a henna-red that God never dreamed of. Her plain black silk dress was sedate and proper, but she wore enough rings, bracelets, and necklaces to make Tiffany's check its inventory.

"I take it we have Jack the Ripper running loose in our establishment, Pierre," she said. "Well, don't stand there gawking. Come in and tell me about it."

I've described Victoria Haven's penthouse in more than one of my stories about Chambrun and the Beaumont. The first impression was of total disorder, a crowded storage place for junk. There was twice as much old-fashioned Victorian furniture in the living room as it could comfortably contain. Heavy red velvet drapes shut out the world, day and night. Bookcases overflowed into stacks of volumes on the floor, along with a clutter of newspapers from God knows how far back. When you recover from your first sight of this apartment collection of rubble, you make an astonishing discovery. There isn't a speck of dust or dirt anywhere. The entire apartment is spotless. What appears to be disorder is obviously complete order to Mrs. Haven. Ask her for a political cartoon from the op-ed page of the *New York Times* from ten months back and she will reach out, probably not moving from her chair, and produce it for you. She knows exactly where anything she cherishes is located.

"I'd about decided to drink alone," Mrs. Haven said. Her voice is husky from too much liquor and too many cigarettes over the decades, but it has a kind of intriguing rasp to it. "Martini, Pierre? As I recall, Haskell, you're a Jack Daniels man—on the rocks with a splash of water?"

She didn't wait for either of us to answer, but strode off to the kitchen. I thought I might help with ice and started after her. My way was instantly blocked by a snarling, obscene little Japanese spaniel, threatening to take my leg off just above the ankle.

"It's all right, Toto. Haskell is a friend," Mrs. Haven called from the kitchen. The monstrous little dog obviously didn't believe a word of it, but he stood aside, an "I'll-get-you-next-time" look on his snub-nosed face.

"Make your own drink like a good boy, Haskell," Mrs. Haven said. "The Daniels is on the counter there. I'll handle the martinis. Pierre likes his straight up, I take mine on the rocks. Tell me about the girl."

"There's nothing much to tell," I said, "except that she's been through a triple nightmare."

"Pierre doesn't go along with the police?"

"Not so far."

"According to the television she may have had dealings with a drug merchant, a sex peddler, and pops off policemen without blinking an eye."

"One thing is certain, she didn't 'pop off' a policeman," I said. "The rest, I'd say, was unlikely but, so far, not proven either way." I poured a generous slug of Jack Daniels over ice.

Mrs. Haven, a cigarette dangling from the corner of her brightly rouged mouth, was stirring Chambrun's martini. "When you've lived as long as I have, Haskell, you learn that people change, and change, and change over the years. I was born in 1900. In the eighty years since then I have been at least five different women."

"I'd love to have known them all," I said, smiling at her.

"Flattery will get you anything," she said dryly. "The problem is there isn't anything left to get." She looked a little sad, I thought, as she stirred Chambrun's martini in a glass pitcher.

"Charming company," Chambrun said from the doorway. Toto had let him follow me without a single snarl of protest. He and Chambrun were obviously more than nodding acquaintances.

The old lady looked at him. "I have a distant but personal interest in this case, Pierre," she said. She took a frosted glass out of the icebox and poured his drink. He took it, toasted her with a gesture, and sipped.

"Perfect beyond my dreams," he said.

"I've been making them for you for thirty years. I ought to know how," she said. She took a step closer to him. Amongst the jewelry she was wearing was a silver chain around her neck with a magnificent emerald pendant attached. "You remember seeing this before, Pierre?"

"You have so many lovely things," he said. "I don't think . . ."

"You haven't seen it because I haven't worn it for, would you believe, fifty-nine years? That's thirty years before I knew you, Pierre."

"Dear Victoria," he said, "there is so much churning in this place that needs handling at the moment. Be a love and make it a short story."

She made a snorting noise and poured her own martini over ice. "No good story is ever short," she said. "I heard about your Valerie Summers on television, and I dug this emerald out of an old jewel case. It seemed appropriate."

"Must I tease you to get to the point?" Chambrun asked.

"When I was eighteen I was a show girl, dancing in a nightclub over near Columbus Circle. 'Monique's' it was called. It was in the summer of the last year of World War One."

"I have heard you had legs that would put Betty Grable and Ann Miller to shame," he said, smiling at her.

"They were good! They were damn good," she said. "I . . . I was just finding out about life in those days, life and love, and all the sensuous pleasures that go with youth. Young men brought me flowers, and jewels, and—and their wonderful maleness. Oh, I played the field, gentlemen."

"That's the one I'd like to have known," I said.

"I don't want to haggle with you, Haskell, but I must tell you the competition would have been pretty fierce. Most of it would have come from the man who gave me this emerald."

"Let's see, the romantic hero of the day was Douglas Fairbanks, Senior," Chambrun said.

"The man who gave me this emerald was Jeb McCandless," Mrs. Haven said.

That was a score! Chambrun stared at her, his eyes narrowed.

"Valerie Summers' father?" he asked.

"You know of some other Jeb McCandless?" the old woman said.

"Well, we seem to have gotten to the point," Chambrun said. "McCandless was eighty-nine years old when he died in 1977. So he was twelve years older than you. Is that important?"

"When you're eighteen a man of thirty is an 'older man,'" she said. "At thirty Jeb already owned half the world. He could buy anything he wanted, and he wanted me. And I could be had. I have been a 'kept woman' all my life, Pierre, in one form or another. That first time it was not for Jeb's money, his power; I was just mad for him as a man, as a partner in bed. For two years there was nothing else in my life, and then I was just simply discarded."

"That's hard to believe," I said.

"Jeb's passion in life was conquest," she said. "Outwitting the competition, winning the new game, taking what belonged to someone else. I never saw him again after we parted, except on the Movietone News, and later on television. But I didn't forget him and he didn't forget me. Bring your drinks."

She turned and walked briskly out of the kitchen. The rooms at the back of the penthouse were just as cluttered as the living room. One of the bedrooms was, literally, just a storage space without furniture. There were dozens of cardboard cartons carefully tied shut. Mrs. Haven bent down, untied one of the boxes, and opened the cover. Inside the box were packages of letters, fastened together with faded colored ribbons. The old lady straightened up and faced Chambrun.

"Letters from Jeb McCandless," she said. "Five years after our thing was over, he began to write to me. Once a month for fifty-two years. Can you believe it? Well, you have to because they're here." She gestured at the cartons. "He didn't want me back. He wasn't a man who would try something over again that had once failed. He had already married and been divorced when the letters started to come. He had loved me, he had made an irretrievable mistake in leaving me, there was no use trying again, but he wanted me to know that he was thinking of me always. Fifty-two years, over six hundred letters."

"Why are you telling us this, Victoria?" Chambrun asked. "Just because his daughter, from a late marriage, is involved in a violence across the roof from you? It is a coincidence, but it's unlike you to be open about something so private."

"Those letters, you could say, contain the story of Jeb McCandless's life," Mrs. Haven said. "His triumphs, his rare defeats, his temporary loves, and the one he thought was finally it, cut short by the birth of a daughter who became the only thing on earth that mattered to him. It's all there, Pierre; how he protected her, how he guarded her by setting up a sort of police state of his own, how she tried to kill herself because he had taken all the joy out of her life, how he finally let her go and appeared to have won out in the end."

"I still don't know why you're telling us this, Victoria," Chambrun said.

"My God, Pierre, do you really think there's no connection between Jeb McCandless's ruthless life and what's happening to that girl? Somebody's trying to punish him, even after he's dead, through her."

"I find that farfetched, Victoria," Chambrun said.

"You're the one who talked about 'background,'" I said to him. "We don't need to go to Tucson. We've got it all here."

"Someone Jeb hurt, crushed, destroyed," Mrs. Haven said. "Someone the girl innocently hurt through having the use of Jeb's money." She turned away, her face a strange, painted mask. "I can't bear to go through these again, Pierre. But if you, or Haskell, or Miss Ruysdale—or anyone you trust, wants to have a look at them, they're here. They're yours. It's the least I can do for a man I once loved."

Chambrun stood silent, his drink hardly touched in his hand. Then he looked at me.

"I'll have a go at it," I said, "if you say the word."

He gave me a tight, mirthless smile. "The last twenty-five years after Valerie was born. That's only three hundred letters, Mark."

A life's work, I thought.

IT WAS THAT TIME OF DAY in the Beaumont when people came into the various bars for the first after-work drink of the day. We had other people's regular customers that afternoon. Three murders, possibly committed by a glamorous heiress, attracted customers like moths to a streetlight. It wasn't the charm of our public rooms, the skills of our bartenders, the courtesy of our maitre d's. We stepped out on the mezzanine balcony, Chambrun and I, when we came down from the roof.

"Ghouls!" Chambrun said. He resented seeing business improved by something he hadn't planned.

Betsy Ruysdale and Maggie Madison, her stand-in, were in the outer office. Ruysdale was studying the list of messages Maggie had taken.

"Three, I would guess, of some importance," Ruysdale said. "Lieutenant Keegan wants to be notified when you are available." That seemed like a new approach to me. The Black Irishman was asking! "Mike Maggio says it's important to talk to you. Something about Willie Bloomfield, the dead man in Five A. And Walter Hardy wonders if you'd like to talk." That was a surprise. Hardy is a Homicide cop from our precinct area. He'd probably have been in charge of the murders at Beaumont if they hadn't been linked to Keegan's earlier case on Tenth Street.

"I'll take them in that order," Chambrun said. "You'd better come in, Mark. Keegan will be dishing out instructions."

Keegan had a right to be dead on his feet. He'd been on the go for two nights and days, but he showed no signs of lost energy. He was wearing a pair of tinted glasses, which suggested his eyes might have revealed the extent of his fatigue. Otherwise he was freshly shaved, wearing a just-pressed suit, and not in love with us.

"We've got to get the rules straightened out, Chambrun," he said.

Chambrun was at his desk, toying with a demitasse of his Turkish coffee. "Whose rules, Lieutenant?" he asked, dangerously quiet.

"My rules!" Keegan said. "I don't object to Mrs. Summers being here in the hotel."

"Your options?" Chambrun asked.

I was tempted to tell Keegan to "look out!" He was playing with a rattlesnake who didn't rattle.

"I could, of course, place her in protective custody," Keegan said. "All her lawyers couldn't do a damn thing about that. But I prefer to have her here because I have to be here. She's either a murderess with a partner-in-crime, or she's being framed by someone who intends to get her one way or another."

"You've come a long way, Lieutenant," Chambrun said.

"She didn't kill Polansky," Keegan said. "It could be her gun, handled by her partner. It could be Polansky caught someone trying to frame her. Either way the man we're looking for will be back. He knows where she is, and he'll try to get to her."

"You mentioned rules, Lieutenant."

"Those other two penthouses on the roof."

"One is occupied—and owned cooperatively—by an old lady."

"Mrs. Haven?"

"Right."

"The other, I understand, is leased by the U.N.," Keegan said.

"You're very thorough, Lieutenant. There's nobody in it at the moment and I intend to keep it that way until this particular storm has passed."

"Good. There's just the one elevator that goes all the way to the roof?"

"Yes."

"That's the only way to get there?"

"Fire stairs. They open out onto the roof behind the U.N. penthouse."

"Why wasn't I told about them?"

"I don't know who you asked, Lieutenant. Not anyone connected with the hotel or you'd have been informed."

"I haven't sensed a feeling of happy cooperation from anyone in this joint!" Keegan said.

Chambrun smiled at him. "'Ask and ye shall receive,'" he said.

"Okay. You've got one of your security people running that one elevator that goes to the roof. I want one of my men in the car with him at all times."

"No problem," Chambrun said.

"You tell me the people who get to use that elevator and, if I approve, my man will have a list and they're the only people who will get to use it."

"I live there," Chambrun said. "I am one of the people who will use the elevator. While Mrs. Summers is there she'll need to see her lawyers, Gardner Fails and Andrew Lukens." Keegan was making a list on the back of an envelope and he nodded. "My secretary, Miss Ruysdale, Haskell here, and Jerry Dodd may need to get to me."

"And that's it?"

"Yes."

"What about the old lady?"

"She must be free to come and go, of course," Chambrun said. "And Toto."

"Who the hell is Toto?"

"Her dog," Chambrun said.

"I suppose she's got a lot of old biddy friends who go up there to gossip and play cribbage and stuff like that?"

"I think you should ask her, Lieutenant."

"You can count on it," Keegan said, quietly boiling. "Now here's the way it is, Mr. Chambrun. My man on the elevator with your man. Two of my men will patrol the roof. You want men of your own up there, so have Dodd identify them. I don't want anyone telling my men he's hotel security and have it turn out to be a phoney. That's what could have happened to Polansky. There'll be two men on the fire stairs. You want men of your own there, have them identified. I know the people on your list. I'll have to be satisfied about any people on Mrs. Haven's list. There aren't going to be any more killings, Chambrun."

"I'm glad to be reassured," Chambrun said.

"You might call Mrs. Haven and tell her I'm on my way up to see her," Keegan said.

"A word of warning, Lieutenant."

Keegan turned back, scowling.

"Toto doesn't like strangers," Chambrun said.

KEEGAN, IT APPEARED, was doing his job. True, there was something of "the locked barn after the horse is gone" about it, but Valerie was my main concern and, I thought, Chambrun's. No matter what his disposition, there was no way Keegan could have foreseen the first two killings. Polansky, on guard and prepared, had somehow been the victim of a sucker punch. Not Keegan's fault.

Keegan had only just left when the little red light blinked on Chambrun's phone. It was Ruysdale to tell him that Mike Maggio was waiting.

Out of his bell captain's uniform Mike looked a little bizarre: a gaudy plaid shirt, pink slacks, white buckskin shoes, and a navy-blue beach jacket draped over his arm.

"Dressed for a wedding, Mike?" Chambrun asked.

"Dressed for a job, if you give it your okay," Mike said.

"You're on the trail of Willie Bloomfield," Chambrun said.

"Ruysdale told you," Mike said.

"Your clothes told me, Michael. You wouldn't be seen in the locker room here dressed like that if you were coming to work."

"I'm supposed to go to work in an hour," Mike said. "I'd like your permission to be a few hours late. Johnny Thacker, the day captain, has agreed to cover for me."

"Let me have it, Michael." Chambrun was already sounding impatient.

"You keep your eyes shut, Mr. C.," Mike said, "but you know as well as I do that some of our most famous and important guests require the services of call girls."

"So?"

"Someone has to see to it that only the best class of flesh peddlers get into our sacred halls. Someone has to screen them."

"You," Chambrun said. The whole subject irritated him. He doesn't like the thought of gentlemen away from home using the Beaumont as a base for fun and games with expensive prostitutes. He also knows that it is a fact of hotel life everywhere. Let a girl on the scene who might have tried to shake down a guest and Mike Maggio would have found himself washing dishes in a spaghetti joint somewhere. Chambrun trusted Mike at a job he wished didn't exist.

"Willie Bloomfield tried to get some of his street tarts on our list a few years back," Mike said. "I made the hotel off limits to him. But here he was last night, got in, got up to Five A, and nobody saw him."

"Not impossible," Chambrun said.

"Not likely, unless we've got a rotten apple in our barrel somewhere. You saw the way he was dressed, Mr. C., strictly Times Square. He couldn't have got into our men's room without being noticed. If he bought somebody on my crew I want to know. Over in Willie's territory the tongues must be wagging like you wouldn't believe. Carl Rogers, the guy who got it the night before on Tenth Street, was part of Willie's world. I thought if I just sat around a few places I might hear something. Buy a few drinks for a few people and who knows what may float to the top— about my rotten apple, if there is one—about this whole mess.''

"Keegan must have that area crawling with under-cover cops and decoys with the same idea," Chambrun said.

Mike laughed. "Street people can spot an under-cover cop a mile away, especially when they suddenly flood a district. They know me in Willie's world. They know I work here and may be able to add something to what they already know. Trade a little dirt."

"You know some dirt, Michael?" Chambrun asked.

Mike grinned. "I can write a hell of an interesting script," he said.

Chambrun made a decision. "Take a flier at it, Michael," he said. "But keep one thing in mind. A killer may know who you are and guess why you're there. If you get too close to him remember that this one doesn't wait for discussions."

Lieutenant Walter Hardy, Homicide, was not new to the Beaumont or to Chambrun's office there. I have described him somewhere else as looking like a "slightly confused linebacker" on a professional football team. He has the guts, the strength, the energy, but he can't quite make up his mind where the attack is coming from. It's not really a fair description. I have watched him work side by side with Chambrun in our violent times at the hotel. We have them, like any other small city. Chambrun is mercurial, intuitive, a hunch player whose hunches almost always pay off. Hardy's slow, plodding, endlessly patient in his search for facts. The hare and the tortoise; Chambrun arriving at answers without the proof, Hardy coming slowly along behind and making Chambrun's case stand up. Hardy would chide Chambrun about his "conclusion-jumping," and Chambrun would nag at Hardy for "taking forever," but actually these two were a mutual admiration society, based on an unshakable mutual trust.

"This is not official, Pierre," Hardy said as Ruysdale ushered him into the office early that evening, "so if you are too busy...?" He smiled a greeting at me. Big, broad-shouldered, blonde, Chambrun once said of him, "If he's handling a rapier have no fear, but if he's armed with a baseball bat or a length of iron pipe, run for your life!"

"Come in, Walter. Never too busy for you," Chambrun said. "It's nice to see someone who doesn't need explaining."

"You finding Matt Keegan a little hard to get along with?" Hardy asked. He sat down in the green leather armchair beside Chambrun's desk.

"Let's say Keegan and I haven't found the footing for a love affair yet," Chambrun said. "I wish you were on the case, Walter."

"I'm concerned with it personally but not officially," Hardy said. "Joe Polansky was a friend of mine."

"I'm sorry," Chambrun said.

"We worked together when I was a detective, first grade," Hardy said. "He wasn't a man to be caught with his pants down. Maybe you can tell me more than I've been able to dig up on the fringes. If I go to Keegan, he'll think I'm trying to get into his act."

"A man who wants the star billing, your Keegan," Chambrun said.

"He's a good cop, Pierre," Hardy said, "but pride does get in his way a little. His father, Jerry Keegan, was a captain and top man in Homicide when I came on the force. His older brother, Marty, retired, disabled after he was shot up in a gang war in Chinatown. Tough cop. Matt married Polly Malone, daughter of Pat Malone, the deputy commissioner, who's my boss. Police on both sides. Fine records. I went to that wedding. Matt announced he was going to have five sons and that they'd all be cops, carry on the Keegan name." Hardy's smile faded. "Polly had a miscarriage trying to bring the first one into the world. No more kids. Matt changed into a hard-driving bastard after that. He's going to be king of the hill, with Pat Malone's help. His record is tops, but he can't afford to mess up a case like this that makes all the headlines. It may make him work a little too hard, a little too eager to come up with the answer in a hurry. He may trip a few times, but he'll make it. You'll see."

"I hope you're right," Chambrun said.

"The Polansky thing bothers me," Hardy said. "He wasn't just a dumb flatfoot, who would let himself be distracted by a pretty maid. He was a detective on a murder case. Nothing was going to take his mind off his business."

Chambrun glanced at me. "I said something like that earlier on to Mark."

"Tell me what your people know, Pierre," Hardy asked.

Chambrun shrugged his expressive shoulders. "Mrs. Valerie Summers is a client of Gardner Fails,

who is on my board of directors. He brought the lady
here after Carl Rogers, a drug pusher, was shot to
death in her West Tenth Street apartment. We put her
up here, and the first evening she's here a sex peddler
is shot to death in her suite. Your man Keegan is convinced the lady is some kind of drug-sex nut, involved in a war with suppliers who know she's a very
rich woman and are trying to rip her off. Could be the
way Keegan thinks, not the way Mark thinks." He
gave me a tight little smile. "The lady has beautiful
blonde hair and dark, mysterious, and possibly passionate violet eyes. She has to be innocent from
Mark's perspective. So—we move her out of the second murder spot, and after the passage of some twelve
or fourteen hours—the lady was given sedatives to get
her some sleep—we come up with a third murder, this
time your Sergeant Polansky. But this time, no matter what the color of her hair or eyes, Mrs. Summers
is, whether Keegan likes it or not, innocent. She had
slept out her sedation, dressed, and gone up to my
penthouse with her lawyers. Miss Ruysdale had spent
the night with her. When the room was empty she
called maid service and suggested that was a good time
to do up the room. The housekeeper sent the floor
maid at once to do the job. Polansky let her in to
1216."

"Joe identified her? She couldn't have been a
fake?" Hardy asked.

"No fake. With us some twelve years," Chambrun
said.

"She had the right kind of mops, Polansky told
me," I said.

"Told *you*?" Hardy looked surprised.

"Mark is the key witness who clears Mrs. Summers," Chambrun said. "A little after noon he went up to the twelfth floor hoping to get a glimpse of those violet eyes. The maid was in the room. Polansky was at his post in the hall. Everything serene. About an hour later Mrs. Summers, her lawyers, a couple of Keegan's men, and Jerry Dodd and one of his security men came down from the penthouse. Polansky wasn't at his post in the hall. Jerry Dodd and one of the cops went into the room and found him there, the side of his head blown off."

"Damn!" Hardy said softly.

"Keegan is summoned, the homicide crew goes to work. A cop named Dawson finds the murder weapon, a small, pearl-handled gun, tucked away in Mrs. Summers' lingerie in a bureau drawer. Ballistics says that gun killed all three victims. Mrs. Summers say she doesn't, never has, had or owned a gun. True or false, she did *not* fire the shot that killed Polansky. At that time she was up in the penthouse, surrounded by her two lawyers, two cops, and two of our security people."

Hardy was scowling down at his big hands, closed into fists on his knees. "Dawson is a good man, solid detective," he said. "I've talked to him. I suggested Joe Polansky could have been shot out in the hall, dragged into the room. No chance, Dawson says. There was so much blood Joe couldn't have been moved anywhere without leaving a trail. It happened in the room, nowhere else. Joe dropped where he was shot. His own gun was in its holster. He never got it out. That suggests to me he went into the room with someone he thought had a right to be there. He was relaxed, unprepared for trouble."

"Who?" Chambrun asked.

"That's why I'm here, Pierre—to ask you that. Housekeeper? A maintenance man?" His brief smile was tight-lipped. "You? Mark, who says he was there and chatted with Joe? You could have asked to go into the room to get something for the lady. Joe would have let you in, followed you, totally unprepared for trouble. You shoot him, plant the gun on the lady, and saunter off."

"You are, of course, not serious," I said. "If I thought you were I'd ask why I'd be planting the gun on Valerie?"

Hardy shrugged. "Maybe she said no when you wanted her to say yes."

"And killed three guys I never saw before just to annoy her?" I asked. "Incidentally, I never laid eyes on Valerie until she checked in here yesterday. I don't take a no so seriously so soon, Walter."

"Of course I'm not serious," Hardy said. "I was only trying to make the point that Joe Polansky could only have been in that room, relaxed and off guard, with someone he thought had a right to be there."

"How about you, or Keegan?" I said.

"Sure. But let me tell you, Mark, if either Keegan or I wanted to plant a gun on the lady we'd have told Joe to stay out in the hall. Being a good cop he'd have obeyed orders from a superior."

"If you children are through playing 'Let's suppose,'" Chambrun said, sounding impatient. "You may, quite innocently have been right on target, Walter. I've been suggesting all along that the killer may have been some man to whom the lady gave a casual no sometime in the past. A no to sex or a no to money. But that doesn't answer your question about Polansky, does it? I think you should consider the possibility, Walter, that no one's perfect.''

"Meaning?"

"I keep repeating myself but nobody listens," Chambrun said. "Polansky had to go to the bathroom, and rather than leave his post he went into 1216. He saw something he thought should be reported to Keegan, and rather than leave his post he went into 1216 to use the phone. Not being perfect, he didn't lock the door behind him. Somebody watching, took the opportunity to follow him in. Polansky may never have seen who it was, it could have been that quick."

Hardy sat silent, trying to put it together that way. Chambrun glanced at him.

"There is a lady up in the penthouse, Mark, whose memory needs cultivating," he said. "If that doesn't work there are six hundred letters that may give us a clue!"

IT WAS ABOUT seven o'clock when I left Chambrun's office and headed down the second-floor corridor to the private elevator. I wanted to avoid the lobby, because I knew the joint would be jumping down there, reporters still hungry for any kind of handout, guests and friends eager for something to add spice to the gossip. I didn't have any spice to offer.

I didn't know it then, had no way of knowing, that the three brutal and cold-blooded murders that had turned our lives upside down were just a prelude to a lesson in terror I wouldn't have believed possible. If I had chosen to go down the hall to my office to pick up any messages my secretary might have left for me before she called it quits for the day I might have avoided what lay ahead. There was a message from Derek Newton, my crippled friend, asking me to call him. He had said it wasn't urgent so my girl hadn't tried to track me down to give it to me. If I had happened to call Derek at that point in time, the whole story might have had a different ending. I didn't know that, of course, and Derek didn't know that he had in his hands the control of a ticking bomb.

Keegan's rules were in effect. When I rang the private elevator bell on the second floor the car came up, occupied by two men. One of them was a strange cop, in uniform; the other was one of Jerry Dodd's security boys who knew me well. I had to satisfy the cop that I was on Keegan's "free list." It wasn't enough for the cop that Jerry's man identified me. I had to produce my wallet with my driver's license and credit cards. He was finally satisfied that I wasn't a phoney and they took me up to the roof. I asked them if anyone else had gone up to the penthouse. No one had.

On the roof there was another strange cop who insisted on going through the same routine. Across the roof I heard a sound like a tiny buzzsaw at work. I realized it was Toto, Mrs. Haven's little spaniel, snarling at us from inside her garden fence. In the twilight I could see a couple of plainclothes cops, pacing slowly up and down. Toto resented them. I didn't. Keegan had the whole place tightly covered. No mad killer was going to find his way up here to get at Valerie. It was a comforting thought.

The cop outside Chambrun's penthouse opened the door for me and I went into the vestibule.

"Paul! Is that you?" Valerie called out from the living room.

I went in and found her standing by Chambrun's piano, leaning on it for a prop.

"Oh, Mark!" she said. "I'm so glad it's you."

"I thought Spector was here with you," I said. I glanced at the chair where he'd tossed his Stetson hat when he'd come in. It was gone.

I crossed over to Val and to my surprise she was suddenly in my arms, clinging to me. That didn't make me unhappy.

"Easy does it," I said. Her blonde hair smelled like honey.

"I . . . I can't bear to be alone," she said.

"I thought the cowboy would never let you out of his sight," I said.

Her laugh was a little hysterical. "He rolls his own cigarettes," she said. "He ran out of the little papers he uses."

"End of the world," I said.

"For him," Val said. "He had to go get some. The policeman outside told him he couldn't get back up without permission from Keegan. He wasn't on Keegan's list. Paul shouted at him that no cop was going to keep him from coming back. That was about an hour ago."

"If he couldn't find Keegan he couldn't get up here with a bulldozer," I said. "Come on, love, sit down. We've got things to think about, like dinner, and your glamorous past. Chambrun still wants to know where you were a week ago last Thursday."

I led her around to the couch and sat down beside her, one of her cold hands in mine.

"Paul is—is something!" she said, turning her head from side to side. "It goes way, way back to when he was—was interested in me."

"'Hungry for you,' is the way he put it to me," I said.

"His idea of how to get me through this difficult time was to...to make love to me!"

I laughed. "But he ran out of cigarette papers?"

"He could be patient, he said, but not without something to smoke."

She laughed too, and I was holding her hand, her head on my shoulder.

"I thought I was going to be raped!" she said.

"His way to make you feel safe," I said. "You say the word, when he comes back I won't leave you alone with him. Meanwhile, if you can trust me..."

"Oh, Mark!"

"There's all kinds of liquor in the cabinet over there if you want a drink. There's certainly something in Chambrun's refrigerator if you're hungry. Most important of all, we have to talk. Somewhere, if we can dig it out, there must be a clue to all this horror. If we just keep talking it may pop out in the open. I saw an old friend of yours earlier today."

"I keep telling you, Mark, I have no friends."

"Derek Newton," I said.

"Oh my God, poor Derek. You know him? You saw him?"

"Your cowboy may have strange ideas about how to provide you with peace of mind," I said, "but I think he's really fond of you. He mentioned Derek, and by a coincidence he is an old friend of mine. I went to see him—looking for a week ago Thursday."

"How is he?"

"He's made a way of life for himself," I said.

"You know that he was in love with my friend Eleanor Payson?"

"He told me."

"I've always thought it was Eleanor's man who beat him up so dreadfully. I tried to see him after she died, but he wouldn't do more than talk on the telephone."

"He told me about you, too," I said.

She lifted her head and looked at me, a faint color mounting in her cheeks. "You mean...?"

"Yes, love. Your Eleanor must have been really something for Derek to turn you off," I said.

"I was twenty years old and still a child," she said. "It was the most shameful moment of my life. To ask him—when I knew so little. Knew *nothing*!"

"He remembers it with tenderness and regret," I said. "It was a lovely thing to happen to a nice man. If he hadn't been a nice man he'd have taken you up on it. If he had, who knows, you both might have lived entirely different lives. I can't imagine making love to you and then going somewhere else."

"That's the way it is with me now," she said. "After five years with Dick Summers I can't imagine turning anywhere else."

"That town in Ohio where you and Dick lived. Surely you had friends there, Val."

"We had friends," she said. "It was Dick's town. They were his friends and they accepted me. I think I fitted in pretty well. I interested myself in community things. There was a theater, and an art gallery, and a hospital. There was always the damned money that I had to find a way to use without their knowing it was mine. That was Dick's big hang-up. They mustn't know I was a McCandless, or we'd be surrounded by people with their hands out. After Dick died, and who I was became known, they reacted as though I'd cheated them!"

"How did you work it—before they knew?"

"Oh, I said I had a friend who worked for a foundation. I got them grants for various things. Of course it was my money. Afterward they thought they should have had twice as much twice as often."

"Was there a foundation?"

"Was and is," Valerie said. "The Hanson Foundation, named after my mother. But it's actually my money. I am 'it,' you could say."

"The Hanson Foundation had to have said no sometimes. Was there somebody deeply disappointed? Did some project collapse without your help? Was there anger somewhere along the way?"

"Something that would lead to three murders and an effort to scare me out of my life and destroy me? Nothing remotely that important to anyone. Honestly, Mark."

"Since you've been living here in New York, has anyone tried to con you out of money? Tried to blackmail you?"

"Blackmail suggests I have something to hide. I don't, Mark! Nothing. And nobody has tried to sell me the Brooklyn Bridge, if that's what the word *con* means."

"So let's let the money go for now," I said. I'd never really seen it as the motive. Killing people wasn't going to get anyone money they wanted. I knew, though, that I wasn't keeping Chambrun's theory quite in focus. A psychotic looney was trying to punish Val, involve her in murder, watch her go through the torture of arrest, conviction, and prison for life. The motive could seem inconsequential to sane people, like no to money or no to sex. What else was there that Val could have refused someone?

I looked at her, lovely, almost relaxed, a look of childlike puzzlement on her face. Was it possible she was a fine actress? Could Keegan have been right from the start, and was she the one who was off balance? Not possible, because she hadn't killed Polansky. Or could there be what Keegan called a 'partner in crime'? Was it possible she could be involved with drugs and Willie Bloomfield's perverted kind of sex? Every instinct I had refused to accept those possibilities. I wanted to say, "Oh, hell, let's forget it and have a drink, and let someone else look for answers." But Chambrun was counting on me.

I did suggest a drink, however, and she chose to have a little white wine and I made myself a Jack Daniels. It was pleasant being there with her. Daylight was almost gone and I could see the lights at the top of the Empire State Building as I made the drinks. We were safe, surrounded by the law. No homicidal maniac was going to find his way to us.

I took the drinks back to the couch and sat down beside her again. I almost had to bite off my tongue to keep from starting on a new tack which could lead to— What the hell, I was no better than the Tucson cowboy. I was telling myself that making love to this beautiful girl was the best way to solve her anxieties.

"Your cowboy told me quite a lot about you," I said.

"I suppose you could say he watched me grow up. Except that I didn't. Not till I was twenty-two years old and I met Dick Summers."

"Your father kept you out of touch with the world, Spector says."

She nodded. "I can't really blame Daddy, when I look back on it," she said. "His wasn't a real world either; not one that you, or I, or anyone else I know knows—unless I were to count in Gardner Fails. He was Daddy's lawyer, you know."

"I know. Spector says he had quite a yen for you when you were a little girl."

She actually giggled. "I wondered why he was always pinching me, touching me. I didn't know the facts of life in those days, Mark. I...I was ten, eleven, twelve."

"After that?"

"A little too overboard with a hello and goodbye embrace when he came to Tucson. Beyond that, a perfect gentleman."

"He never made an outright pass at you?"

"Good Lord, no! And yet..."

"Yes?"

"I've come to realize, as I look back, how close he must have come to risking his life, his future, his fortunes with Daddy. Daddy would have killed him if he'd guessed that Gardner had any sort of romantic interest in me."

"Your father seems to have kept you away from the facts of life," I said, "and yet he'd had no scruples living it up himself. Four wives, God knows how many side bets. Would you believe that just across the roof from here in Penthouse C there is a fabulous old lady who was his mistress sixty years ago?"

"Mark!"

"She has over six hundred letters from him to prove it," I said.

"Who is she?" The violet eyes were very bright.

"Victoria Haven. I don't know what her name was when your old man picked her out of a nightclub chorus."

"How fascinating!"

"I've been offered a look at the letters in the hope they might throw some light on all this mess."

"How could they?"

"Everybody's playing wild guessing games," I said. "Mrs. Haven thinks someone may be trying to punish your father, even after his death, by trying to destroy you. That's one of a hell of a lot of guesses we're playing with."

She was silent for a moment, letting that sink in, a tiny frown creasing her forehead.

"If she knew my father down through the years, I can see why she'd make such a guess," Val said finally.

"She never saw him after they split up. They had, I gather, a torrid two years. But he started writing her after a while, once a month for fifty-two years!"

"He must have cared for her."

"She's quite a gal," I said. "Even now, at eighty."

"I told you my father's world wasn't a real world," she said. "As a child I supposed every child was as closely guarded as I was. As I began to grow up I realized we weren't like other people. For Daddy there was a mortal enemy hiding behind every sagebrush. He thought I would be the target. I would be kidnapped and they would gouge him for his whole world." She gave me a bitter little smile. "There came a time when I decided it wasn't me he cared for, but the things he owned, the things he controlled."

"And so to the hot bath and the razor blade?" I said.

She moved away from me, her eyes wide. "Paul really did talk to you, didn't he?"

"He said it was no secret. Everybody at the Tucson place knew."

She nodded slowly and held out her arm, pulling back the sleeve from her wrist. I could see the little white, crisscrossed scars from long ago.

"My own silly melodrama, played in my own silly way," she said. "Right out of some French novel I'd been reading. But it turned out to be a lucky event."

"Oh?"

"It revealed to me that Daddy really loved me, truly loved me. You see, none of the things he feared evaporated for him. The danger to him through me was still there. But if I was so desperate about the way he'd patterned my life, then he would face it, take the chance, set me free. He cared for me that much, and it made my world over."

"He made you change your name?"

"That was the only precaution he asked me to take. I thought I'd look around and find one of his men dogging me, following me East to college, that he'd try to guard me without my being aware of it. He didn't. He played it dead on the level, and oh how I loved him for it!"

"And nobody ever did make a move against you?"

"No. For a while I lived in fear of it, expecting to be grabbed and carried off in a great black limousine by Arab oil sheiks. Nothing ever happened, and the world I found outside Daddy's 'fence' seemed so wonderfully free, and exciting; people my age of both sexes, brilliant intellects like—like Derek Newton, books, theaters, just to walk down the street in the town of Poughkeepsie without anyone keeping tabs on me."

"And the time had come when you had to say yes or no to the young men in your world," I said.

She gave me an almost shy look. "I was so green, Mark. Maybe I said no without even realizing I was saying it. I knew... I knew there was something stirring in me that I had to satisfy. But it wasn't I who said no. It was poor, dear Derek. I was so ashamed, and so turned off, that a whole year went by. And then...then I met Richard Summers. There was no saying yes or no. It just happened, wonderfully, magically. It never occurred to either of us that we wouldn't be married, until Dick found out who I really was, the rich Miss McCandless! It almost ended it. But once again my father was an angel. He set aside his anxieties about a 'fortune hunter' and assessed Dick for what his real worth was."

"He knew you were having an affair with Dick?"

"He wasn't a fool, Mark. I must have been as transparent as glass. He must have known it would happen when I went East. I was a late-blooming woman." She reached out and touched my hand. "You and Mr. Chambrun keep suggesting someone is out to get me because I said no to them. There was never anyone, Mark, who came close. This seems to be a time for no secrets. I have never made love to any man, or come close to making love to any man, but Dick. The idea of someone else, while Dick was still alive, never even crossed my mind. Afterward . . ."

"There was someone?"

"No. I knew, though, that a reasonably attractive widow with no ties would be fair game. I didn't want to face it then, not ever I sometimes think. That's why I came to New York and shut myself away. I didn't want to encounter it in even the most casual way."

"And you didn't?"

"Didn't." She gave me a long, steady stare.

"Do I want for you to ask, or do I ask?" I said.

She stood up and walked quickly over toward the French windows. I had meant what I'd said to be a light kind of crack, something to laugh at but keep in mind! She had evidently taken it quite seriously.

I don't know how Val might have responded because, at that moment, there was the most unwelcome of interruptions. Lieutenant Keegan, the Black Irishman, walked into the room, unannounced.

THREE

OBVIOUSLY KEEGAN SAW ME but he acted as though I wasn't there. His dark, scowling attention was focused on Val who had turned back from the French windows, aware of some new presence behind her.

"We're going to have to talk some more, Mrs. Summers," Keegan said.

I could see Val stiffen. She took an uncertain little step to the right where she could reach out to the back of a chair to steady herself.

"I've told you everything I have to tell you—over and over," she said, her voice unsteady.

"Over and over, if you haven't got it memorized, has a way of bringing up a little something new each time," he said. "I've been going over your statements, taken down by a police stenographer. There are still things that don't check out." He took a notebook out of his inside pocket. In the movement involved I caught a glimpse of the holstered gun under his left arm. He turned a couple of pages in the notebook. "The night before last, when Carl Rogers was shot in your apartment, you say you went to the theater. The name of the show again."

"*Sugar Babies*, with Mickey Rooney and Ann Miller," she said.

"The theater?"

Val hesitated. "I . . . I don't recall. It's on Broadway, in the early 50s."

"The Mark Hellinger Theater, Broadway and 51st Street," Keegan said. "You told us you didn't see anyone there you know."

"I don't know a dozen people here in New York, Lieutenant," she said. "Is it so surprising none of them was at *Sugar Babies* that night?"

He ignored her question. "You don't have a ticket stub to prove you were there," he said. "What happened to that stub?"

"I . . . I don't know."

"What do you usually do with ticket stubs when you go to the theater?"

She gave him a blank look as though she didn't understand what he was getting at.

"When I go to the theater," he said, coldly quiet, "I hand my ticket to the man at the door, he tears it in half and hands me back my stub. I give my stub to an usher who takes me down the aisle and points out my seat. He hands me back my stub and I put it in my pocket. Why do I keep it?"

She looked flustered. "In . . . in case . . ." she said.

"In case someone else claims my seat," he said. "In case, if I go out for a cigarette in the intermission, I'm not dead sure where my seat was. The chances are I don't discard that stub until I empty my pockets before I go to bed that night. What do you do with your ticket stub, Mrs. Summers, after the usher has shown you your seat and handed it back to you?"

"I suppose I . . . I put it in my purse," Val said.

"You looked in your purse that night when we first questioned you," Keegan said. "No stub."

"I know."

"So what did you do with it?"

"I told you then, and I tell you now—I just don't remember."

"Threw it on the floor in the theater?"

She sounded desperate. *"I don't remember!"*

He turned a page on his notebook. "We have a police photograph of you, Mrs. Summers, taken the night before last when we were summoned to your apartment. We took that photograph to the Mark Hellinger Theater. Not a single person in the box office, not the ticket taker at the door, not one of the crew of ushers remembers ever having seen you."

"A couple of thousand people every night," I said. I'd had enough of this. "A couple of thousand *different* people every night. Val isn't a movie star. Why should they remember?"

He turned on me, and his eyes were as cold as two newly minted dimes. "I let you stay here, Haskell, because her lawyer isn't here. I don't want her telling someone I brutalized her. But you keep your mouth shut or out you go." He faced Val again. "Where did you buy your ticket for the show, Mrs. Summers?"

She moved slowly around the chair she'd been clinging to and sat down on it. "I don't think you will want to understand," she said.

"Try me, Mrs. Summers."

"That night...that night I was restless, Lieutenant. I wanted to get out of my apartment, shake the thoughts I'd been thinking."

"What thoughts?"

"For God's sake, Lieutenant, it's only eight months since my husband was burned to death! Sometimes, thinking about it is almost too much to bear! I went out, with no particular plan, thinking I'd find a movie or perhaps a play that would take my mind off it. I'd seen the movies in the neighborhood theaters. I took a taxi up to the Times Square area, knowing I'd find something to see.''

"You take the cab number?"

"No!"

"So we won't be able to find him, will we?" Keegan said. "Go on, Mrs. Summers. You still haven't got a ticket to *Sugar Babies*."

"I paid off the taxi—somewhere in the Times Square area. I just walked, looking at the theater marquees. I found myself outside a theater—you say it's the Mark Hellinger. There was a big picture of Mickey Rooney. I remembered him with pleasure in the movies, so I thought I'd try. It looked pretty hopeless. The lobby was crowded. There was a line to the box office but people seemed to be turned away. I was about to try somewhere else when a man came up to me. Did I want a single ticket? He had one I could buy. Orchestra seats were twenty-two dollars, I think. This man wanted fifty dollars for his.''

"And you bought it?"

She nodded.

"What a McCandless wants a McCandless gets," Keegan said. He sounded outraged. "I don't suppose you could identify this ticket scalper if you saw him again?"

"I might," Val said. "I'm not sure."

"So we have a whole evening accounted for, without a shred of proof to back up any single part of it," Keegan said. "I thought going over and over it you might remember something that would check out."

"Where were you a week ago Thursday at two o'clock in the afternoon?" I heard myself asking Keegan.

"What the hell are you talking about?"

"I just wondered if your memory is any better than Mrs. Summers," I said.

Keegan pointed a finger at me like an angry schoolteacher. "One more smart-ass crack out of you, Haskell, and you're gone!" He turned his back on me as though he needed me out of his sight in order to control his temper. When he finally spoke to Val again I was surprised to hear something that sounded almost like sympathy in his voice. The tough cop and the friendly cop is an old police routine. It involves two investigators, one of them demanding, angry, accusing, and the other playing the "I'm your friend" side of the street. Keegan obviously was going to try to play both sides.

"I have a job to do, a murderer to catch, Mrs. Summers," he said. "I have to play the cards as they fall. If you could remember a single thing about night before last that would check out, verify a single detail of where you were and what you did, I could turn somewhere else. I don't have a passionate desire to prove you guilty. If I could prove you innocent it would do just as well. As it is, I have to keep hammering at you. Do you understand?"

"I...I'm too tired for it to matter," Val said. It was almost a whisper.

"So we have to keep at it. Let's forget about the night before last for now, and go to last night."

Val lowered her head and covered her face with her hands. I wanted to go to her, but I thought Keegan would use that as an excuse for ordering me out.

Keegan turned the pages of his notebook. "After Rogers was murdered in your apartment, Mrs. Summers, your lawyer, Fails, brought you here to the Beaumont. You were set up in suite Five A. That was early afternoon. Two o'clock?"

"It may have been," Val said.

"At six-fifteen Haskell turned up to invite you to dinner. There is a gap of four hours and fifteen minutes about which we know nothing. I want to fill in that gap, Mrs. Summers. You weren't being watched or guarded then. Unfortunately we didn't guess that there was more to come. So let's try to account for that four hours and fifteen minutes. Did you leave Five A during that time? For lunch? For something you may have needed in the drugstore or one of the shops?"

Val shook her head slowly.

"To meet a friend? To make a call on a pay phone you could be sure wasn't monitored?"

"No! I never left the suite."

"Who came in to see you during that stretch of time?"

"No one."

"You just sat there in the suite for four hours and a half?"

"I . . . I was exhausted. I tried napping but it didn't work."

"You make any phone calls?"

"No."

"You're positive?"

"If she made any out-calls there'd be a record of them at the switchboard," I said.

Keegan gave me his black stare. "Last warning!" he said. "You look at television, Mrs. Summers?"

"I tried to get news on the TV a couple of times," Val said. "I thought there might be something about ... about Tenth Street."

"And did you get news on the TV?"

"Yes. But nothing about Tenth Street."

"What station?"

"I don't understand."

"What station did you tune into?"

She turned her head from side to side, as if she was coming to the end of her endurance. "I ... I just switched the set from channel to channel until I found someone with news."

"Man or woman?"

"Man—I think."

"What was the news at that moment?"

"About the hostages in Iran—and something about the Russians in Afghanistan. What does it matter, Lieutenant?"

"If I knew what channel you'd tuned to, I could find out what they were broadcasting at the time you say you were watching. That could substantiate one single statement you've made about key times in the last two days. It's extraordinary, isn't it, that nothing you've told me about night before last and last night can be backed up by a witness, by a material fact like that ticket stub, by anything at all?"

Val stared at Keegan as though he made no sense.

"He slipped and fell," she said.

"Who slipped and fell?" Keegan asked, darkening.

"Mickey Rooney," Val said. "In a dance routine. He covered it up, wonderfully, making it look as though it was intentional. But the audience knew, and they applauded. I'd have to have been there to know that, wouldn't I, Lieutenant?"

"We're talking about last night," Keegan said. He was moving over from being the 'nice guy,' back to the Inquisition. "Tell me one thing I can take hold of that will help me account for four hours and fifteen minutes of your time!"

"If you asked Mickey Rooney he would tell you that he slipped and fell in one of his dance routines," Val said.

"That was night *before* last!" Keegan almost shouted. "We're talking about two o'clock to six-fifteen *yesterday*!"

Val lifted her hands to cover her face again. She'd had it, I thought—in spades.

"Nobody with your kind of money—fifty dollars to a scalper for a theater ticket!—lives the kind of nothing life you say you've been living, Mrs. Summers," Keegan said. "No friends, you say. People with your kind of dough always have friends, or people who pretend to be friends. You isolated yourself so you could grieve for your dead husband, you say. People like you can afford to go to a shrink when they have troubles. Have you been going to a psychiatrist?"

Val just shook her head, slowly, warily.

"What does a woman in your situation do?" Keegan said. "I thought drugs when I identified the dead man in your apartment. The hotel doctor, Dr. Partridge, says there's no indication that you're a drug user. He had to make sure when he gave you sleeping pills, after we'd found Willie Bloomfield dead in your bedroom in Five A. You could afford to buy it by the bushel from Willie. Willie and Carl Rogers worked together. Not drugs, not sex, you say. So what were they up to, each of them in a place where you lived? I think I have the answer to that, Mrs. Summers. Those two characters had a sideline which they worked very successfully—until night before last and last night. Blackmail! What did they have on you, Mrs. Summers?"

Valerie looked up. It was a final effort, I thought.

"I never saw either of them before," she said. "I never heard of either of them before."

"Maybe you just paid off a messenger boy," Keegan said. *"What did they have on you?"*

She lowered her head again, face covered, and began to cry softly, her shoulders heaving but almost no sound.

"I'm on target, right?" Keegan said, sounding triumphant. "They had something on you, raised the ante, and you shot them both in cold blood. What was it that would drive you to go so far to keep hidden?"

At the opportune moment I heard the front door to the penthouse open and close. I've seen someone move quickly in my time, but Keegan took the prize. The gun under his left armpit came out so fast he'd have made an old-fashioned gunslinger look paralyzed.

The interrupter was Detective Dawson, the cop who'd found that little pearl-handled gun in Valerie's bureau drawer. He gave Keegan a frozen little smile.

"Hey, point that thing some other way, Lieutenant," he said.

Keegan held the gun dead-steady. "What the hell do you mean walking in here?" he demanded. "I'm involved in an interrogation."

"If you'll come outside for just a minute," Dawson said.

"When I'm through!"

"It's your ball game," Dawson said. He gave me a kind of odd look, I thought, and then he turned and went out. I heard the front door close behind him.

"Now, Mrs. Summers," Keegan said, slipping his gun back in its holster, "let's have a little truth for a change."

"There is nothing, nothing, nothing, that I haven't told you," Val said. "Must I invent something to please you? For God's sake, Lieutenant!"

The phone rang. I was standing right next to it and I picked it up before Keegan could say a yea or nay.

"Mark Haskell here," I said.

"Mark? It's Chambrun." His voice sounded tense. "Can you bring Mrs. Summers down to my office?"

"No."

"You're not alone?"

"No."

"Keegan?"

"Yes. He's interrogating Valerie."

"Mark, play it very cool," Chambrun said. "Keegan may turn out to be our man."

"What man?"

"The killer," Chambrun said. "If he is, he's way overboard, and you and Mrs. Summers are in big trouble. We'll get to you as soon as we can."

The phone went dead. My hand felt frozen to the receiver when I tried to put it down.

"Who was it?" Keegan asked.

"Chambrun," I said.

"What did he want?"

My mouth felt dry. "An invitation to dinner for me and Mrs. Summers—when you're through," I said.

He gave me a twisted little smile. "I hope you're not too damned hungry," he said, "Because I'm not anywhere near through."

It was like somebody telling you the ice was too thin to support you when you're already out in the middle of the lake. I tried to remember Chambrun's exact words. *"Keegan may turn out to be our man.... If he is, he's way overboard, and you and Mrs. Summers are in big trouble."*

I stood there by the phone, feeling as if my feet were nailed to the floor. I couldn't move, as I watched Keegan turn back to Valerie. He was a nice-looking, well-dressed, highly thought-of policeman. Hot tempered and aggressive, yes, but a killer? A man who had shot one of his own police officers? A man with a psychotic obsession to destroy Valerie Summers—or Valerie McCandless? What possible connection could there be between a highly rated homicide detective, member of an Irish family of respected cops, and a Midwestern housewife—or a Southwestern heiress? Surely Val had never seen or heard of Keegan before he came on the scene to handle a murder in her apartment two nights ago or she would have told us.

I hadn't liked Keegan from the first moment I saw him. It was the instinctive reaction to a man who used his muscle and his power position to push you around.

Jerry Dodd had called him a "sonofabitch" but given him high marks as a cop. Lieutenant Hardy had backed up that assessment.

"Keegan may turn out to be our man."

Coming from anyone but Chambrun I'd have laughed that off. Too far out. There were, though, a couple of little things. There was the lightning speed with which Keegan had produced his gun when he heard someone unexpected come into the penthouse. There was the warning look Detective Dawson had given me before he pulled out. *"We'll get to you as soon as we can,"* Chambrun had said.

What was stopping them? All they had to do was get on the elevator, come up to the roof, and walk in. I knew the answer almost as I asked myself the question. If Chambrun was right, Valerie and I were hostages in the hands of a crazy man!

Keegan was sitting on the end of a stretcher table, looking down at Val, huddled in an armchair. He reached inside his jacket and took out that police special once more. He put it on the table, just an inch or two away from his right hand. He turned his head and gave me that tight, cold little smile of his. He didn't say anything, but he might just as well have told me that he knew I'd been warned.

"I guess the time has come to stop playing games with you two," he said, focusing on Val.

"I don't understand," Val said.

"Chambrun told me on the phone," I said, "that Keegan may be the killer."

"Not 'may be,'" Keegan said. "Can you understand, Mrs. Summers, how deeply and forever I hate your guts?"

Her wide, violet eyes gave him a dazed looked. "I don't know you! I *don't* understand," she said.

"Haskell, get Chambrun on the phone again," Keegan said. "When you get him bring the phone to me."

I hesitated and I saw his hand move toward the gun. I picked up the phone, asked for Chambrun, and heard Ruysdale's voice.

"Mark here, Betsy," I said. "Keegan wants to talk to the Man."

"Hold on," Ruysdale said.

The phone has a long cord on it and I carried it down the table to Keegan. He took it, so I couldn't hear Chambrun's voice, couldn't speak to him.

I could only hear Keegan's end of the conversation. It went something like this: "Chambrun? You turn out to be a wise guy, friend.... I'd love to know how you found out, but we don't have time for that now.... Let me tell you how it is. Mrs. Summers is sitting about three feet away from me. I have a gun, as you must guess. Three feet is like shooting fish in a barrel.... Yes, I'll tell you what I want. I want the elevator that comes to the roof with no one on it. It can run automatically, can't it? ... I want the cops on the roof and on the fire stairs called off duty.... Ask your friend Hardy. There are a dozen men with authority to give that order.... When the coast is clear I will take Mrs. Summers onto the elevator and down to the garage in the basement.... Yes, the garage.... I want a car waiting, no one guarding, no one watching. You can stop me, of course, but if you try I will blow the lady's goddamned blonde head off her shoulders.... Yes, I know it will take time to arrange all that. But not too much time, Chambrun. Not too much time.... You call me, here, when everything is set.''

He put down the phone and slid it back along the table toward me.

"You just stay still and keep your mouth shut, Haskell," he said, "or they'll find you here, like they found the others, when Mrs. Summers and I have gone. Is there any bourbon whiskey in that cabinet?"

I couldn't find a voice to answer. I just nodded.

"Pour me a slug," Keegan said.

I went over to the sideboard-bar, found some Early Times, poured about three ounces in an old-fashioned glass. The neck of the bottle rattled against the rim of the glass as I poured. He pointed to a spot on the table, just beside the gun. I carried the drink to him. Any decent American hero, I thought, would put down the drink, snatch the gun, and shoot him right between the eyes. I guess I'm not a decent American hero. He had me hypnotized with those bright black eyes of his. I put down the drink and backed away.

"I'm sorry," I said to Valerie. "It was just not worth the risk."

Keegan laughed. "You disappointed me, Haskell. I thought for sure you'd try."

"When you know you're going to die," I said, "it isn't sensible to speed up the process. However, it would be nice to know why."

"Mrs. Summers knows why," he said. He took a swallow of his drink. "Before she pays for what she's done I'm going to make her sweat, and sweat, and sweat—until it gets to be a bore. I thought it would be satisfying, Mrs. Summers, to see you arrested for murder, see you tried and convicted, and know that you'd spend the rest of your life in jail with those locked-up harpies clawing at you. Women in prison like to foul up the pretty newcomers. No way the McCandless money could buy you out. No more sex. Well, it will be quicker this way. But before I'm through with you, Valerie McCandless, you will be praying for me to put this gun to your head and pull the trigger."

"What have I done to you?" Valerie whispered.

"You destroyed everything that ever mattered to me," he said.

"What is it they used to say on 'Mission Impossible'?" a hoarse voice asked from behind us. "'This tape will self-destruct...'? You are a master at self-destruction, Lieutenant."

FOUR

I SPUN AROUND. Keegan, gun in hand, faced the
French windows. We were confronted by something
like an apparition. I have heard Chambrun, in a gently
affectionate mood, refer to Mrs. Victoria Haven as the
Madwoman of Chaillot. Mrs. Haven was an everyday experience for me, striding across the lobby, Toto
under her arm. To Valerie, who didn't know her, she
must have looked like something out of a romantic
childhood fiction. The henna-colored hair was piled
up on her head with some sort of jeweled Spanish
comb set at the back. Toto, her miserable, sneering
little spaniel was tucked under one arm, and a woven
straw bag, probably a shopping bag, dangled from the
other. A bright-colored paisley shawl was draped over
her shoulders, partly obscuring the glitter of rings,
bracelets, and necklaces she was wearing. Behind her,
framed in the doorway, were the tower lights of the
city. A great stage director couldn't have designed a
more dramatic entrance.

Keegan's gun was pointed directly at her ample
bosom. Toto, the black-and-white Japanese spaniel,
gave him a nasty look and snarled at him.

If Victoria Haven saw the gun she gave no sign of it.
I wondered if vanity kept her from wearing glasses.
She must be blind to wander into the room with that
gun pointed directly at her. But wander in she did,
plopped herself down on the couch, placed Toto on

one of Chambrun's upholstered cushions, opened her straw carryall and from it produced a long ivory cigarette holder, a package of Camels, and an old Zippo lighter. Her gnarled fingers were remarkably agile as she fitted a cigarette into the holder, lighted it, and dropped the cigarettes and the lighter back into the straw bag. She gave us a kind of triumphant smile.

"Nasty habit," she said, and blew a perfect smoke ring toward the ceiling. "Well, let's see, where are we?"

I daresay that was one of the very few times in his life that Matthew Keegan had been caught completely by surprise.

"This is police business, Mrs. Haven," he said. "I must ask you to leave."

"Oh, nonsense, Lieutenant," the old woman said. "We all know it isn't police business, don't we?" She reached down in the straw bag and produced some knitting. The wool was a garish scarlet color. It was a sock, set up on steel needles. She began to knit, not looking at what she was doing, obviously quite expert. "I learned to knit socks a long time ago," she said. "It was 1917 or 1918, I think. Just toward the end of World War One. It was supposed to be the patriotic thing to do, for our gallant doughboys overseas. I used to knit everywhere; in public restaurants, on the streetcars, backstage at the nightclub where I was performing. I thought the whole world would see that I was a person of character." She paused, took the cigarette holder out of her mouth, and didn't quite make the ashtray on the end table beside her. She gave Valerie a pleasant smile. "I used to knit socks for your father, my dear. He was in love with me, you know, so he had to wear them, something the doughboys were not compelled to do. I've often wondered if that may have been the beginning of what led to our breakup."

"Mrs. Haven," Keegan shouted at her.

"Oh, dear, I'm just rambling on, aren't I?" Toto growled, startled by the loudness of Keegan's voice. "Naughty Toto," she said. "Mr. Keegan used to be a policeman, and policemen know how to deal with naughty little dogs."

"I am a policeman, Mrs. Haven," Keegan said, "and I want you out of here on the double."

"Oh dear me, Mr. Keegan," she said, "you stopped being a policeman quite a little while ago. Pierre called me a few minutes back, you know. I was to evacuate my premises, by way of the fire stairs, and get the hell off the roof! No," and the needles clicked on, "I don't like to be given orders, even by Pierre, who is an old and trusted friend. He told me that you were the killer and that you were holding Mark and this lovely young woman hostage. Well, I've never been held hostage by a handsome Irishman, Mr. Keegan, so I thought I'd join the party." She gave him a dazzling smile.

I could almost hear the wheels turning in Keegan's head. His gun was aimed straight at her. Just a little squeeze on the trigger and that would be that. I couldn't guess what his plans for Valerie were—a trip somewhere in a car to where he would have her all by himself. Mrs. Haven was a nuisance, and it didn't matter how many more murders he undertook. The roof may have been destroyed by the police, who were no longer his men but his enemies, but it was certain they weren't very far away. The sound of a shot would imply to them that there was nothing to wait for, no reason to hang back. They would move in.

"You do know this is a gun I'm aiming at you, Mrs. Haven," he said.

"Of course I know it's a gun. I grew up with guns, Mr. Keegan."

"You do know that all I have to do is squeeze the trigger and that's the end of living for you?"

"I'm in my eighty-first year, Mr. Keegan. I've long ago adjusted to coming to the end of the line," Mrs. Haven said. She smiled at Valerie. "Your father taught me to use a gun sixty years ago, girl. He was a marvelous marksman. He could hit a ten-cent piece at fifty paces. Shooting from the hip, no aiming."

Keegan took a step toward the sofa. Instantly Toto was off his cushion, bouncing up and down like a rubber toy, shrieking his outrage. The little dog's reaction was so violent that Keegan actually made a small backward move.

"Now, now, Toto," Mrs. Haven said. "Manners!"

Toto sat back down on the cushion, snuffling and growling.

"Let's see, where was I?" Mrs. Haven said, the steel needles clicking away. "Ah yes, your father and his marksmanship. Your name is Valerie, isn't it?"

Val nodded. I think we all, even Keegan, must have looked like kids watching a magician perform his miracles on the vaudeville stage. Nothing that related to reality seemed to penetrate Mrs. Haven. The movement of those needles was magic. It had to be magic that prevented her from seeing a gun that was pointed straight at the center of her smiling face.

"I shouldn't have to ask you your name, my dear," Mrs. Haven said to Val. "For twenty-odd years you were a large part of a once-a-month letter to me from your father. Let's see, you had a buckskin cow pony named Gilly?" Val nodded. "And a Dalmatian dog named Spot? I don't remember his ever mentioning guns in relation to you. He never taught you how to use one?"

"No, Mrs. Haven," Val spoke with a kind of wonder. This fantastic old woman had been her father's mistress sixty years ago!

"Jeb obviously changed with the years," Mrs. Haven said. "He set you down in a fortress and surrounded you with an army. He taught me to defend myself. There was a pistol range in the basement of his house. We spent hours there while he taught me to shoot with my right hand, my left hand, over my shoulder at someone coming at me from behind. I got to be damn good." She turned her smile on Keegan. "Do you suppose I'd still be any good, Keegan? Is shooting something you don't forget, like how to swim?"

Keegan looked as if he couldn't believe what was happening. I suddenly realized what *was* happening. Victoria Haven was, ingeniously, using up time; time for Chambrun and the police to plan what their move would be. The needles clicked on and the talk rattled on, throwing Keegan just enough off stride so that he couldn't proceed with his own plan, whatever it was. I had an absurd impulse to applaud!

"When you were born, Valerie, Jeb could use an army and a fortress to protect you," Mrs. Haven said. "You were his child. He could openly protect you. I was his lover, his bed-partner, back in 1920. He was married then to his first wife, Eloise. Rich men were expected to have mistresses back in those days, but they weren't supposed to be open about it. They used to say that a good marriage was made in heaven, but your father's marriages, except to your mother, Valerie, were made, you might say, on the Stock Exchange. Your father married three women, before your mother, all of whom were the daughters of big power figures in the world of giant corporations. Jeb needed those men and they needed Jeb. Loveless marriages helped to cement those business connections. I can tell you, though, Valerie, that if Jeb cared he could be a marvelous lover. I held onto him for two years, and I can say that there was nothing afterward that could touch him.''

"I think we've had about enough of your life history, Mrs. Haven," Keegan said. He turned to me. "Get Chambrun on the phone."

"You know what it's like to marry for power, don't you, Keegan?" Mrs. Haven said, needles clicking away. "Your father-in-law was supposed to take you to the very top, wasn't he? If you hadn't blown your stack you'd be headed there today, wouldn't you?"

I had moved the telephone down the stretcher table to where he could reach it, but he didn't seem to notice it. I picked up the receiver and asked the switchboard to get me Chambrun. Keegan reached out, took the receiver away from me, and put it down on the phone, cutting off the call.

"I wonder if you were as good a lover outside the bonds of matrimony as Jeb was?" Mrs. Haven asked him.

"Just what the hell do you think you're babbling about?" Keegan demanded. Toto was up again on the cushion, snarling.

Mrs. Haven touched the dog and he subsided. "I'm talking about you, Keegan, and what drives a good, competent Irish cop off his rocker. Haven't you wondered how Chambrun got onto the truth about you?"

"It doesn't really matter any longer how," Keegan said. His bitterness was so intense I could almost feel his pain and anger.

"It's extraordinary, isn't it?" Mrs. Haven said, "how the best laid plans of mice and men can be derailed by coincidence."

The phone rang. Keegan picked it up. "Yes, Chambrun, I was trying to reach you.... Yes, I know you said it would take time, but not all night, pal.... I don't want to play games, Chambrun. I don't want to talk to any hostage-rescue team. I know all their routines. It would be a waste of time.... I have another hostage, by the way. That crazy old woman who lives across the roof from you just wandered in. Talk, talk, talk.... Yes, Mrs. Haven.... She gives me another card to play, if you don't start moving.... If you can persuade her to get the hell out of here."

He reached out and handed Mrs. Haven the phone, just missing having a finger taken off by angry Toto.

"My dear Pierre," Mrs. Haven said into the phone, beaming at the three of us as though it was Christmas and we were all sharing in a call from a favorite uncle. "Yes, my dear, of course I'm here. Otherwise how could I be talking to you?...I know... I know... But you know how difficult it is for me not to be where the action is.... Yes, I know. He is, I'm afraid, a very disturbed young man.... I was about to tell him how you came to find out about him, but he seems to resist the idea. He must be curious, don't you think?''

Keegan leaned forward and the barrel of his gun actually rested against the old woman's cheek. ''Tell him I expect him to have a car ready in twenty minutes. No more time.''

''Knowing that you're not deaf I suspect you heard Pierre.... Well, I'll try to keep him entertained while you get things ready, Pierre.... Oh, my dear, don't be concerned. I'm having a ball!''

She handed the phone to Keegan and he put it back on the table.

''You're in for a big surprise, Mrs. Haven, if you think this is some kind of game,'' Keegan said.

''There are games and games,'' Mrs. Haven said, turning the scarlet sock and starting along a new row of knit one, purl one—or whatever. ''There are games you play for fun, and games you play for high stakes, and games you play because you're sick and self-destructive.'' She gave him an interested look, like a parent dealing with an erratic child. ''Making a game of punishing Mrs. Summers for what she did to you is completely self-destructive. You'll never be able to take a step out into the daylight again, out into the civilized world. Is it really worth it?''

''Damn you, you old bag!'' Keegan said, under his breath.

''Now, now, Keegan. Sticks and stone, sticks and stones,'' she said.

''What have I done to him?'' Val cried out. She was sitting up in her chair, her eyes wide. ''I never saw him before in my life till the other night—in my apartment—when he came to investigate."

"Fascinating, isn't it?" Mrs. Haven said. "He wants to punish you for something you don't know you did. Let me make a rather grim suggestion to you, Valerie. It might be the better choice to die here than to let him take you somewhere else and drag it out, slowly, painfully."

Val slumped back in her chair, hands raised to her face again. I had to go to her, gun or no gun. I moved around to her chair, knelt down beside her, and took both her hands in mine. I looked at Keegan's dark angry face. I didn't say anything but he knew I was suggesting he get it over with if that's what he wanted.

"You're really quite amazing, Keegan," the old woman said, needles clicking. "You really don't want to know how Chambrun got to know? You don't want to know what mistake you made? If I were you I just couldn't stand not knowing, whatever I planned to do later. Incidentally, is a good, brutal rape a part of your scheme for Mrs. Summers? I confess it puzzles me how a man so full of hate could perform sexually. I suppose it's a special kind of sickness."

"I've had it from you, lady," Keegan said. "Just keep still if you want to stay in one piece." He glanced at his wristwatch. "Fourteen minutes. Can you keep still that long?"

"Talking is a compulsion with me," Mrs. Haven said, "like violence is a compulsion with you. You've left one question unanswered, but I suppose you must have been a good lover or Eleanor Payson wouldn't have stayed with you for so long."

"Eleanor!" I heard Val whisper.

"You didn't know, did you, my dear?" Mrs. Haven chattered on. "Neither did anyone else until just a little while ago. Keegan was your friend Eleanor's married lover. He was the father of her son. He must have been quite an exceptional lover. She stayed with him—what was it, Keegan, six, seven years?"

Keegan took a step toward the old woman. He wasn't aiming his gun at her now, but had it drawn back as though he meant to slash her across the face with it. She sat perfectly still, even the steel needles stopped clicking. Her bright old eyes gave him a steady stare, as much as to say "I dare you!" He didn't strike her and the needles started clicking again.

She looked at me and I must have been white as a ghost. "I mentioned earlier, Mark, that coincidence could upset the best-laid plans. A press photographer took a picture of Mr. Keegan with reporters crowding around him in the lobby sometime yesterday. Either you didn't get a message that Derek Newton had called you, or you thought the call wasn't important."

"Derek?" I said, through lips that didn't want to work. "I didn't get any message."

"A bad mischance, or things might be different. For years Derek tried to find out who Eleanor Payson's lover was. He saw the man once, leaving Eleanor's apartment—sometime before the terrible beating that put him out of circulation." The bright, pale eyes flickered Keegan's way and then came back to me. "Derek lost the man that time in the crowded city traffic, but the fact was etched on his memory. This afternoon he saw that picture, printed in the evening *Post*. The caption under the picture indicated that the face he'd looked for so long belonged to Lieutenant

Keegan of Homicide. He called you because he thought it must be a mistake. He thought you could tell him which person in the picture was really Lieutenant Keegan, and to ask if you knew the man who had, he thought, been wrongly identified in the *Post* picture. When you didn't call back he phoned Pierre. There was no mistake in the picture. It was you, Mr. Keegan, and Derek knew at last who had crippled him for life. Pierre, of course, realized he was no longer looking for a mysterious Mr. X. It was too late, however, to stop you from getting control here. If Pierre had any doubts, Mr. Keegan, you resolved them by blowing your own ball game.''

A nerve twitched high up on Keegan's dark cheek. Holding Valerie's cold hands in mine, I tried to make other pieces of the puzzle fit together. What did Carl Rogers, a drug pusher, and Willie Bloomfield, a sex and pornography peddler, have to do with Eleanor Payson, Val's dead friend? Why had Keegan blasted them and planted them on Val? He had meant to make trouble for Val, the biggest trouble he could, but why had he chosen those two particular men? He had called them blackmailers when he'd been wrangling with Val. Could he, Keegan, have been a victim?

Val was taking deep, almost gasping breaths. I slipped an arm around her and held her close. She turned to look at me, and spoke as though no one else was there.

''Eleanor's lover!'' she whispered. ''But what has that got to do with me, Mark?''

''A sick mind comes up with sick reasons,'' Mrs. Haven said in a casual, conversational tone. I wanted to warn her. If she kept needling Keegan he might give her his full attention for just long enough to squeeze the trigger on his police special. And then I thought, for God's sake, that was exactly what she was trying to do! She wanted to turn him off Val! Sixty years ago she had been in love with Val's father. Was she trying to pay some kind of debt she imagined she owed? Was she thinking that Val had a full life to live and that she was at the end of the line anyway? A romantic kind of guts, I thought. Did she think I might have the brains to do something for Val in the confusion she might create? I looked around, searching for an escape hatch that didn't exist. Keegan could get off a half-dozen shots before we could move ten feet. I didn't want to die trying to be a white knight.

"Why, Mr. Keegan? Why?" I heard Valerie say. Her whole body was trembling like someone with a drill.

The Black Irishman's face was dark with a kind of rage I don't think I'd ever seen anyone feel before. "You meddled in my business, Mrs. Summers. You helped Eleanor get away from me. You helped her steal my son. *My son*, do you understand? What you did resulted in the death of my son, do you understand? You and your money put an end to everything I cared for in the whole world!"

"She didn't pilot the plane, Mr. Keegan," Mrs. Haven said, needles clicking away.

"God damn you, *shut up!*" Keegan shouted at her.

"How was it, Valerie?" Mrs. Haven asked. "Did you advise your friend what to do, or did you just give her the help she asked for? I heard this whole story long ago from Derek Newton. He is my friend as well as Pierre's and Mark's. When he first came out of the hospital, mutilated by you, Mr. Keegan, paralyzed so that he couldn't ever walk again, he used to let me sit with him. I was too old for it to matter to him that I saw him the way he was. I used to think that if I could ever find out whoever did that awful thing to Derek I would be capable of murder."

"If you ever had that chance you've lost it." Keegan said. "Eleanor didn't love Derek Newton. If she had she would have left me long before she settled for me, bore my son. He kept trying to get at her, to steal her—like this meddling bitch! I fixed him, and I'll fix you, Mrs. Summers!"

"It would be fascinating to know what Eleanor saw in you, Mr. Keegan," Mrs. Haven said. "Were you such a marvelous lover that you could turn to beating her, beating *her* son, depriving her of any decent kind of life of her own? That you could hold her prisoner until at the end she found the means to escape?"

"Eleanor did love him," Valerie said, "but he had changed. He wasn't the same man she had given years to."

"He was sick," Mrs. Haven said. "Killer sick."

I thought that was it; she'd gone beyond that point where he was going to take any more from her. He took a stride toward her, and the little spaniel was up on its cushion, snarling.

Then there was a miracle. A great, booming voice called out his name from the roof outside.

"Keegan!'

I realized it was someone calling out through a police bullhorn. Keegan was so quick I couldn't get out of his way, let alone interfere. He grabbed Valerie, wrenched her out of the chair, and stomped over me as though I wasn't there. I rolled over, trying to get my bearings, and saw that he'd dragged Valerie to the left of the French windows, out of sight of anyone on the roof. His left arm was around her throat from where he stood behind her, and his gun was being held against the side of her head.

"Keegan!" the booming voice sounded again. "It's Walter Hardy, Homicide. I want to talk to you."

None of us spoke or moved, except Toto, who permitted himself a threatening growl. Keegan glanced at me. Have you ever seen a madman in action?

"Open that French door so he can hear me," he said.

I got to my feet, somehow, and walked over to the door. The roof was dark. If Hardy was out there I couldn't see him. I could open the door and run for my life, I thought. However deep-rooted my cowardice was I couldn't leave the two women to Keegan, no matter how useless I was. I opened the door and moved back into the room. I stood where Hardy could see me—if he was on that side of the roof. The bullhorn made it impossible to locate him accurately.

"Can you hear me, Hardy?" Keegan called out.

"Clear as a bell," Hardy said, off the horn. He couldn't be more than twenty feet away, I thought. I could hear the distant sound of traffic, the foghorn noise of a ship on the East River. The real world was out there. "We have to talk," Hardy called out.

"No point," Keegan shouted back at him. "I'm holding the girl against the inside wall. My gun is stuck in her ear. Don't try anything, Hardy."

"Is Mrs. Haven all right?"

"I'm fine, Lieutenant," Mrs. Haven called out cheerfully.

"Mark?"

"Okay—so far," I managed to say.

"Cut the chatter!" Keegan said.

"You have to know what the situation is out here, Keegan," Hardy said.

"I don't need to know anything except that the elevator is ready to take me and Mrs. Summers down to the basement garage, and that there's a car there waiting for us," Keegan said.

"That's only a part of the situation out here," Hardy said. He sounded so casual, like an old friend having an unimportant conversation with an old friend.

"There's nothing to understand, Hardy. That elevator will be up here in twelve minutes now. If it isn't—"

"It's not all that simple, Matt," Hardy said.

"Nothing in the whole goddamn world is simple!" Keegan shouted.

He was holding Val so tightly around the neck that I could see the veins standing out on her forehead.

"Ease up on her, Keegan," I said. "She can't breathe."

He must have relaxed his hold a little because I heard a little choking sob come from Val.

"Chambrun can arrange the elevator for you, Matt," Hardy said. "He can arrange the car for you. But he can't set anything in motion because the police are in charge."

"So tell them, Hardy. Tell them to move. If they don't let me get this woman out of here they'll be responsible for her death, and maybe two others."

"Three others, Matt," Hardy said, in that completely unemotional voice. "Once you start killing you're dead yourself, you know. We've got an army in this hotel."

"I don't matter!" Keegan said.

"That's why we need your help in deciding what to do," Hardy said. "You're not going to get away in the long run, Matt, no matter what we do about right now. You're not asking for money to get away, or a plane, or free passage to someplace from which you can't be extradited. You just want time to torture and punish a helpless woman. All you have to do, Matt, is fire a shot, or make the lady scream, and we'll be all over you. In the long run that may be the kindest thing we can do for the people you're holding. I can see Mark where he's standing, frozen. I can see Mrs. Haven. They can't do anything because you will just pull the trigger. But you are going to do that anyway, sooner or later, aren't you, Matt? So why should we simplify things for you?"

Keegan didn't reply or change his position, except to lean his head against the wall. As though the cool feel of the plaster might relax his tensions a little.

"There are two people out here with me who'd like to talk to you, Matt," Hardy said, unhurried, although Keegan's silence must have concerned him.

"I told you, talk is a waste of time, Hardy," Keegan said. "You've got nine minutes to get that elevator up here. That's all—nine minutes!"

"Don't set time limits, Matt," Hardy said. "Just convince me that it makes sense to turn you loose. Just convince me that Mrs. Summers has a better chance if we turn you loose than if we don't. We think if you take her somewhere else it will put off her dying for a while, but that in the end you will kill her. We don't propose to let you put her through that agony. Make us believe, Matt, that there is some way you will let her survive. Two minutes after you've convinced us the elevator will be there. Until you do, there's no chance it will come at all."

"You bastard!" Keegan said.

"I'm not making the decisions, Matt," Hardy said. "The man in charge didn't feel he could talk to you without it becoming too personal."

"Malone?" Keegan asked.

Patrick Malone, the deputy commissioner, was, I remembered, Keegan's father-in-law. Malone was supposed to have been Keegan's way to the top.

"Captain Carmody, Matt," Hardy said. "It would naturally be the precinct captain in this area. You remember he used to be Joe Polansky's partner before he was promoted? He feels pretty badly about Joe, Matt. He feels he couldn't talk to you without his personal bitterness interfering. He stood up for Polansky at his wedding, is godfather to his three kids." Hardy waited for a moment or two for Keegan to respond. Watching, I could see Keegan tighten his grip around Valerie's neck, forcing her to bend back against him to keep from strangling. His gun never wavered from its position against her head. I could imagine how Hardy was thinking. How far could he go? How long could he stall? He was flirting with the danger that something he said could drive Keegan to squeezing the trigger of his gun, and that would be that. From out there on the dark roof Hardy could probably see us all in this lighted room. If there was some way to persuade Keegan to move away from Valerie, turn his attention somewhere else, they might be able to take charge. Play it wrong and Valerie was dead.

"There is someone out here who wants to talk to you, Matt," Hardy said.

"Who?" Keegan said.

"Your wife."

"Oh, Jesus!" I heard Keegan whisper.

"Matthew? Matthew, it's Polly." The woman's voice sounded on the very edge of hysteria.

"Go away!" Keegan cried out.

"Please talk to me, Matthew," Polly Keegan said. "There's so much I...I don't understand. Twenty-four years and it comes to this and I...I don't understand. Dad says to tell you if you'll just stop running, just stop—stop what you're doing—he'll get you the best lawyer, the best care, the best help."

"It's too late for lawyers or help," Keegan said. "Just go away, Polly, and forget you ever knew me."

I thought he sounded genuinely distressed for her. It was the first glimmer of anything human he'd shown up to now.

"They've told me so many things in the last hour that I never dreamed of," Polly Keegan said. "There's a man down in the office—in a wheelchair. They say you put him there, Matthew."

"I put him there," Keegan said. "I didn't mean to. I meant to kill him. I thought I had."

"Matthew!"

"*Go away*, Polly!"

"I never dreamed there was another woman, Matthew. I never had the faintest notion that there was someone else. Your job kept you away often—I thought. I grew up with policemen. I thought I knew how it was."

"I stopped making love to you eight years ago. Did you think I'd taken a vow? Turned into a monk?"

"I thought you knew I was afraid. I thought you were being kind to me."

"Oh, God!" Keegan said.

"Was—was the little boy who died in the plane crash your son, Matthew?"

"Yes, he was!" Keegan shouted. "He was, was, *was*!"

In that moment I thought he was either going to break away from Valerie—or kill her. It was a physical thing with him. What he did was to drag her down onto the floor, his gun still at her head as he knelt beside her.

"You could have told me," Polly Keegan said. "I would have understood. I'd have let you go. Anything but this, Matthew."

"Hardy!" Keegan called out.

"I'm here," Hardy said, sounding ghoulishly cheerful.

"Get her away," Keegan said. "It's too late to explain, to make anything make sense to her. I'm sorry, Polly, but what the hell good is that. Hardy! You've got six minutes to get that elevator up here!"

There was silence. I strained to hear the sound of footsteps on the tarred gravel of the roof. Watching

Keegan, I thought he was trying to hear some sound he could understand. After a bit he couldn't take it.

"Hardy!" he called out at the top of his lungs.

"It's all right, Matt," Hardy said. "She's gone. Your wife has gone." He was so close, just a few feet away, I thought.

"What has Carmody decided?" Keegan demanded. "Does he get me out, or do I start spattering brains on the rug here."

"You still haven't convinced us that Mrs. Summers has a chance if we let you go, Matt," Hardy said.

"Why don't you give up, Mr. Keegan?" Victoria Haven asked from the couch. Her needles were working steadily again. "You could just let Valerie walk out onto the roof where Lieutenant Hardy could get her to safety. Mark could make us a drink while we wait for them to come for you. It would be so much easier than bloodying up the scenery."

"Four minutes!" Keegan called out to Hardy, ignoring the old lady on the couch.

"You've got to give me more time than that, Matt," Hardy said. "I'll have to get to a phone and talk to Carmody. It's his final decision to make. I'll have to check with Chambrun, to make sure the elevator will take you uninterruptedly to the garage, and that a car is ready for you."

"All that should have been set up long ago," Keegan said. "It's not so damned complicated."

"Oh, the elevator and the car aren't complicated, Matt," Hardy said. "The problem is our options."

"You haven't got any options," Keegan said.

"Hardly any," Hardy admitted. "You kill Mrs. Summers here and now, or somewhere else and later.

It's not much of an option, but one we have to consider."

It seemed clear enough to me. "While there's life there's hope." As long as Keegan didn't pull the trigger on his gun there was a chance for Val. I told myself there *must* be a sharpshooter out there on the roof. How long could Keegan last without shifting that gun to his other hand? Just that much change in the situation might give a skilled marksman a chance. They couldn't just tell Keegan to go ahead and get it over with. Surely they must be thinking that between the rooms and the basement garage, getting into a car and driving up the ramp to the street, there would come a moment when Keegan would be vulnerable and they'd have a chance. Captain Carmody was a blank to me, how he would react in this crisis wasn't something I could predict. Chambrun, who must be in on the decision making, I knew better than my own father. He knew his hotel like I know my own face in a shaving mirror. He would know exactly how long it would take that private elevator to go from the roof to the basement. I had traveled it hundreds of times, but I couldn't guess how long it took to travel forty-two floors. Chambrun would know to the second. He would know if in the basement there was a step down, a step up, how close to the elevator they could park a car. He would know where police could conceal themselves, behind a supporting upright, in a tool shop, overhead on a supporting steel beam.

I was convinced they had to let Keegan and his hostage get that far, get to the waiting car, get started up the ramp. Once they were at the top of the ramp and at the street it would be, I told myself, a different decision to make. Once they let Keegan get away with Val she was dead. He was that mad. I knew that from just watching him, listening to him. I had a vision of the car reaching the street level, confronted suddenly by a half-dozen cops with machine pistols, blasting away. There was one chance in a thousand, with the guns all aimed at the man behind the wheel of the car, that Valerie would survive the hail of bullets, the shattering glass, the impact of the driverless car crashing into something on the street. I could imagine Chambrun, that hanging judge look on his face, telling Captain Carmody that one chance in a thousand was better than no chance at all. I was sure that was the way he would see it.

I came out of my dream world to hear Keegan shouting to Hardy on the roof. There was no answer. From where I stood I could see a little trickle of sweat running down Keegan's cheek. Hardy was stringing it out just a little too far, I thought. This lunatic was just about ready to pop his cork.

"Lieutenant Hardy told you he had to consult with his superiors," Mrs. Haven said, knitting away. "He'll be back. Your father used to say, Valerie, that when more than one man has to make a decision Rome could burn before they make up their minds. You haven't made it easy for them, Mr. Keegan. They're damned if they do and they're damned if they don't."

"Just—please—get it over with!" Valerie pleaded.

He gave a savage yank at her and I thought for sure he'd broken her neck. Her head lolled to one side and her body sagged against the wall. But he never took his gun away from the side of her head for an instant. If someone was watching him through a telescope sight

Keegan hadn't given them even a fraction of a second. I saw Mrs. Haven's mouth tighten, but she went on with her sock, as relaxed as if she was waiting for the tea water to boil.

"I'd be fascinated to know just how you would handle this situation, Mr. Keegan, if you were out there in Hardy's place, or in Captain Carmody's shoes with the big decision to make. You were a fine cop before you slipped over the edge. You'd have known exactly what you were going to do, wouldn't you, without waiting to consult or shuffle your feet. How would you handle it if you were out there, Keegan?"

A kind of growling sound came from Keegan, but he didn't answer. The old lady looked up over her sock at me. "How about you, Haskell? How would you handle it if you had Captain Carmody's job?" She was playing games; playing games for time.

"Different ways of handling things," she rambled on, "is what makes a horse race. One small mistake by Carmody and he has lost; one small mistake by Keegan, and he's lost. It's most interesting when you stop to think about it." She looked up at me. "We really don't have anything else to do but think about it, do we, Haskell?"

I glanced at Keegan. A little muscle had knotted along his jaw and it was ebbing and swelling. It was such a close thing now, so very close.

"Two men with the same mentality—in their sane moments," Mrs. Haven said. The steel needle clicked and clicked. "Each trained in the same school, each tutored in the same techniques for crisis situations. Captain Carmody, poor fellow, is at a disadvantage. Keegan knows every step he is trained to take, and he knows Keegan knows. Keegan, he is well aware, has been taught every countermove a criminal might make in such a situation. Worst of all for Carmody, he knows that Keegan has now turned psychotic so there are no predictable actions he may take.''

Needle, needle, needle! If she could jab at Keegan's tender spot enough times he might turn on her to keep her still. In that moment—*if* there was a marksman out there—Val could be saved. We could all be saved. Brinksmanship! What a gutsy old doll!

''How does it go in the book, Keegan?'' Mrs. Haven asked. ''The hostage, or hostages, come first, do they not? Carmody has to wait, hold off till the very last moment, in the hope you may be willing to bargain for Valerie's life. What you have to guess is how long he will wait, how long he will hold off. You hope it will be long enough for you to get that girl somewhere and brutalize her. But can Carmody go that far? They might give you a medal, Keegan, for killing a couple of animals like Carl Rogers and Willie Bloomfield. But you've also murdered a brother cop. They'll never let you get away with that. That seems to me to have been such a stupid thing to do. I don't suppose there's any point in asking you how it happened?''

Keegan, crouching beside Valerie, left arm around her neck, gun in his right hand held to her head; opened his mouth and shouted at the top of his lungs: *''Hardy!''*

''He probably had to go down to the floor below to find a phone. Is that where Carmody would set up his headquarters—one flight down? As close as he can get to this area without frightening you into acting impetuously?''

"His time is up," Keegan muttered. "So help me God . . ." The knot of muscle moved up and down his cheek as if he was grinding his teeth.

"But he will come back, Keegan," Mrs. Haven said. "He knows he can't give you too much time to decide on something he isn't prepared to face. He knows you have the advantage here, because you don't have to consult with anyone. Not your God, because, certainly, you don't have one." A moment of silence, and then: "Can we pass the time, Keegan, by talking about Derek Newton? Imagine what it must be like for him, sitting down in Chambrun's office, knowing that only a trip on an elevator separates him from you. What would you do, Keegan, if you could get a man who had done to you what you did to Derek?"

"What I'm about to do to you if you don't stop babbling," Keegan said.

For one almost unbearable moment I thought he was going to turn on her, and if he did we'd know if there was a marksman out there. It could all end just that quickly—if there was a marksman. But Keegan never once relaxed his attention to Valerie. He could be shot dead, I thought, and his final violent spasm would squeeze the trigger that would end her life, too.

"Truly, a storybook romance," Mrs. Haven was saying. "Poor Derek didn't find the love of his life until she was already committed to the Prince of Darkness. That's a fanciful name for you, Keegan. And how committed! What was it, Keegan, six years, seven years? In all that time never a word to suggest who her lover might be. Not even when she was running for her life, with her son, helped by Valerie's money, did she betray the identity of her Prince of

Darkness. Not even when Derek, a kind, concerned friend, was trying to find a way to rescue her and was crippled for his pains did she disclose her secret. Was that because she now knew that you were violently psychotic? Did you threaten the child's life, Keegan? Is that what sealed her lips forever? She knew you were capable of the kind of insane violence you're caught up in now. I daresay that might have silenced me. It's hard to imagine how a woman must feel watching a man she has loved passionately, tenderly, whose child she had borne, turn slowly into a monster. Maybe she could think of him as sick, mad-dog sick. But by saying nothing she exposed the rest of the world to him.'' Knit one, purl one; knit one, purl one. ''Maybe, if she'd reached the sanctuary Valerie planned for her, she'd have seen the light after a while and rung the bell on you, Keegan.''

''Look over here, old woman!'' Keegan said, in a loud, harsh voice. ''You see how it is? One sharp jerk backward and this bitch's neck is broken. One wrong move, out there on the roof or in this room, and I blow her head off. I know what you're trying to do, lady. Talk and talk, needle and needle. It's a technique I've used a hundred times myself, talking some screwball away from his intentions, distracting him for just long enough. You're good at it, Mrs. Haven, but you've got the wrong sucker.''

The needles had stopped and the old woman sat very still.

''I forget about this bitch and pay attention to you, just for a couple of seconds, and a guy out there with a high-powered rifle finishes me. You asked how I'd handle it if I was Carmody. That's how. I even know the man I'd have stationed out there, Sergeant Spivak, best man on the whole police force with a rifle." Keegan raised his voice. "That you out there, Tommy Spivak?"

Silence.

"That's the way they play it," Keegan said. "No one talks but the main talker. That's Hardy, with an unexpected assist from you, lady. So save your chatter. It doesn't touch me."

As though it was on a prepared cue Hardy called out. "You there, Matt?"

"Where else would I be, Hardy?"

"Carmody has made his decision," Hardy said. "You get the elevator and the car. But there's one condition."

"No conditions!" Keegan shouted.

"Just listen, Matt. The condition works for you. It isn't possible to alert hundreds of people milling around the hotel, lobby level, garage level—coming and going. Someone might make a false move we can't control, seeing you with a gun at the lady's head. Chambrun thinks if Mark Haskell is with you he can clear the way for you. Everybody knows him as representing management. He can talk you past any roadblock. You willing, Mark?"

I felt my heart jam against my ribs. It didn't make too much sense. The private elevator wouldn't stop at the lobby if it was set to go to the basement garage. The police could have the garage deserted if they wanted to. Chambrun had something else in mind than "roadblocks."

"If Chambrun wants it, sure," I said.

"What about it, Matt?" Hardy called out.

"Why not?" Keegan said. "Give me an extra target if Chambrun's trying to play wise guy. But I've got conditions."

"I can't promise," Hardy said.

"I want Tommy Spivak and any other riflemen you have out there pulled off the roof before we go to the elevator."

"That I can do," Hardy said. "Five minutes? And then you head for the vestibule and the elevator."

"Five minutes."

"You go too, Hardy."

"If you say so. One more thing, Matt."

"There's always one more thing, isn't there?" Keegan said.

"The elevator, on this occasion, Matt, is controlled by the engineer in the basement. That's to keep innocent guests of the hotel from stopping it on the way down. But it must also stop you from dreaming an impossible dream, Matt. You can press buttons until they come out of your ears and you can't get it to stop at some floor halfway down—in case you thought of trying that and making a run for it. It will be just as you demanded. Elevator to the basement, car waiting, your move. Okay?"

"Five minutes from now," Keegan said.

"See you around, Matt," Hardy said.

Silence. I glanced at my wristwatch. I thought I could hear it ticking, but of course it doesn't make any sound. That was my heart, banging against my rib cage. Keegan didn't move, but he could see his own watch. It was right in front of him with his left arm looped around Valerie's neck.

"I'm sorry, Haskell," Mrs. Haven said. She had dropped her knitting back in her bag. Her right hand had Toto by his collar. I think she thought the feisty little spaniel might make a pass at Keegan when he started to leave.

"You played a great game," I said.

"When something doesn't work you can't call it great," she said. "If you get to Pierre, tell him I tried."

"One minute," Keegan said. "You lead the way to the elevator, Haskell. We'll be right behind you." Thump, thump, thump, and then he said, "Now!"

If I tell you I thought my legs wouldn't work perhaps you'll understand. I took a last look at old Mrs. Haven, rigid on the couch, cuddling her dog, a last look at Val drooping in Keegan's viselike grip, and walked, almost stiff-kneed toward the vestibule. There was just a small table lamp burning there. Across the six feet of vestibule the elevator waited, door open, lights bright, looking like some sort of eighteen-foot-square oasis. Some jerk had turned on the Musak and, believe it or not, a long-ago Fred Astaire was singing softly, "White Tie, Top Hat, and Tails."

"Go right in," Keegan said from behind me.

I walked in. The car is completely enclosed, air conditioned—and a Fred Astaire concert! I turned. Val was staring at me, terrified, over the top of Keegan's stranglehold on her.

"How do you start it?" Keegan asked.

"Press the 'Close Door' button," I said.

"You press it."

I turned to the control panel and got the door closed. We started, almost noiselessly, down.

"How do you turn that music off?" Keegan demanded.

"I don't know. It's controlled from the basement."

Then it happened. The car stopped. The lights went out and we were in complete darkness except for a little red emergency light on the control panel. That goes on automatically when the power is off. Astaire was gone, too. In his place was Ethel Merman belting out something from *Annie Get Your Gun*. It was deafening in that small space.

"They're playing some kind of a lousy trick on us!" Keegan shouted. "So help me God, I'll . . ."

The lights came on again and the car started down.

"Momentary power failure," I said. I couldn't think of anything else to say.

Merman had shifted to "There's No Business Like Show Business." I don't know whether everyone else is like me, but I have a tendency, when I'm going down in an elevator, to look up to where I've just been. You can't see anything in this totally enclosed car, but I looked up. I don't know what kept me from shouting out, but there was a good-sized square hole in the roof of the car. On the other side of the hole was a face, a stranger. He put his finger to his lips in a gesture to me to keep silent. I almost had to clap my hand over my mouth. The stranger's hand appeared and he dropped something in the car behind us. A little curl of smoke came up from it and I saw it was an old-fashioned string of kid's Fourth of July firecrackers. They went off, snapping and popping.

For the first time in what seemed like hours Keegan spun away from Val, and the man on the roof of the car fired three shots. The total noise in that small space was beyond belief when you added a shrill screaming from Keegan. He did a kind of crazy pirouette, like a ballet dancer in a climactic leap. I think in that last moment he was still trying to get off a shot at Val.

I like to think that I grabbed at his gun arm. At any rate I could see the police special gleaming in the corner of the car. I had Val in my arms, trying to shield her from the sight of the fountain of blood that seemed to come from Keegan's mouth.

Then the elevator door opened and I think there were a million people trying to crowd in at once. The first face I saw was Chambrun's. It felt like waking from a nightmare.

FIVE

IT'S HARD TO MAKE any kind of order out of what happened in the next few minutes.

I remember Chambrun holding out his hand to me, and between us we got Valerie out of the elevator. We were at the garage level. There was a car waiting there—if things had gone that far.

Cops, along with a police doctor, carried the blood-soaked Keegan to an ambulance that pulled in just behind what might have been the getaway car.

I heard Hardy's familiar voice asking the police doctor what Keegan's chances were.

"Early to guess, but not too good, I'd say," the doctor said.

"Maybe it's best that way," Hardy said. He sounded bitter. "The way our courts work these days, they'd probably find him unfit to stand trial by reason of insanity. Couple of years later they pronounce him cured, turn him loose, and he's ready to start on another rampage."

You remember little things like that.

Like Val's fingers locked in mine. "I don't believe it," she whispered to me. "I never thought we'd make it, Mark."

"That makes two of us," I said.

Like Chambrun smiling at an oddly familiar man. "Would you believe, Sergeant, those firecrackers have been in my desk drawer for a couple of years? Confis-

cated from a kid who was setting them off in a flow-
erpot in the lobby. Remembered them at the last
minute.''

"I was praying they'd go off," the man said. "It
worked perfectly."

I knew, then, where I'd seen him before; through
the hole in the roof of the elevator. Later I learned he
was Sergeant Spivak, the expert marksman Keegan
had mentioned—was it years ago?—up in the penthouse.

Like Betsy Ruysdale bearing down on us, grinning
like a Cheshire cat. "Come with me, Val." And Val
turning to me, still clinging to my hand.

"I'll catch up," I said. "I promise."

Like Chambrun taking my arm and giving me his
own brand of victory smile. "This calls, I think, for a
triple Jack Daniels," he said.

I knew damn well I could use it.

Somehow we avoided an army of press people and
got to his office on the second floor. Chambrun
poured me a beer mug full of whiskey on the rocks and
plopped me down in the green leather armchair by his
desk. I took a long swig of the Jack Daniels and began to congratulate myself, privately, on being alive.
Like Val, I hadn't believed we were going to make it.

"Mrs. Haven?" I heard myself ask the Man.

"She's on her way down," Chambrun said.

"Great lady," I said. "She stalled him and stalled
him, tried every way you can think of to get Keegan to
turn on her. Was Spivak out on the roof?"

Chambrun nodded. "All she had to do was to get
Keegan to take that gun away from Mrs. Summers'

head and Spivak would have had him, right between the eyes."

"Keegan knew that, I think."

He nodded. "Time was so important. We had to find a way to stop him before he hit the street. My plan took time to organize, and then sell to Carmody and Hardy."

"Your plan?"

"The elevator," he said. "That's where I thought we could trap him. But we had to cut a hole in the roof and cover it with a piece of lead foil, so he wouldn't notice if he happened to look up when he first got aboard."

"Spivak was on top of the car all the time?"

"My dear Mark, when that elevator goes up to the vestibule outside the penthouse it goes right up to the top of the shaft. If a man was on top he'd have been crushed to death. That's why he had to stop you on the way down."

"Oh my God," I said, "when the light went out and he started shouting—"

"It only took a few seconds for Spivak to climb aboard from the thirtieth floor where he was waiting," Chambrun said. "MacKenzie, our engineer, had the exact spot figured out—to the inch." He smiled at me. "Maybe we owe Ethel Merman an assist. I thought if you were locked in a dark closet with her belting out 'There's No Business Like show Business' you might be distracted for a moment. I owe you, Mark. I felt we had to have somebody along who could give him an explanation when the car stopped and the lights went out, or he might polish off Mrs. Summers then and there."

We were suddenly not alone. Lieutenant Hardy was in the doorway, and beside him, pushing his wheelchair toward us, Derek Newton. Behind him was Mike Maggio, our night bell captain, who, I suddenly remembered, had taken the night off to listen to gossip in the world of porno-sex. And then, charging past them all, was Victoria Haven, a hostile Toto tucked under one arm.

"Not one word till I'm settled and can listen intelligently," she said.

The pieces went together fairly neatly once you had them all. It was Chambrun, it seemed, who had first suggested to Hardy that Keegan might be the man they were after. To Chambrun, it was the only thing that explained to him the murder of Sergeant Polansky in 1216.

"Not a careless man," Chambrun said. "He let someone in the room because that someone was his boss. Maybe he just wanted to talk to someone, maybe he remembered something he thought Keegan should know. He left his post in the hall and followed Keegan into 1216—in time to see Keegan planting the revolver in Mrs. Summers' lingerie drawer. He knew, then, that his boss was the killer. He started to make a move, and Keegan, with that little pearl-handled gun in his hand, had to use it."

"I didn't buy it," Hardy said. "Not for a minute—till Mr. Newton arrived with his picture and his confusion about the caption. The man the photograph identified as Lieutenant Keegan couldn't be Keegan, because Mr. Newton knew he had been Eleanor Payson's lover, and was probably responsible for his being in a wheelchair. That was enough, but Keegan was al-

ready up in the penthouse. We sent Sergeant Dawson
up there to try to get him to come outside but Keegan
wasn't buying. The rest you know."

"When Dawson reported," Chambrun said, "and
I knew we were setting up a siege, I called Mrs. Haven
and ordered her to leave the roof by way of the fire
stairs. It seems," and he smiled, "she didn't buy,
either."

"That girl was Jeb McCandless's daughter," Mrs.
Haven said. "You never read my letters, Pierre—and
you never will, now!—so you don't know how much
he cared for her. I owed Jeb for the best two years of
my life."

"Sixty years ago," Chambrun murmured.

"And every year after that I was a year older,"
Victoria Haven said. "That's what life is all about,
growing older. It should be the other way around,
Pierre. You should spend your life earning youth, not
false teeth!"

"Maggio, here, filled in the missing pieces," Hardy
said. "We knew we had our man, but Maggio helped
us understand what seemed so senseless."

"There was talk all over Willie Bloomfield's
world," Mike said. "There was no reason for anyone
to button up with Willie and Carl Rogers both dead."

It was no longer a secret that had to be kept in Willie Bloomfield's world. It was already on television
that Keegan was holding hostages at the Beaumont,
wanted for murder.

It seemed that a couple of years earlier Carl Rogers, delivering drugs to a customer in the Village, had
witnessed the savage beating of a man in an alley between buildings. Rogers recognized the attacker. He

was Lieutenant Keegan, son-in-law of Deputy Commissioner Malone, a big shot in the department. Rogers passed what he knew along to his partner, Willie Bloomfield. They watched the papers, saw Newton's story, guessed he could identify his assailant. It was all they needed to turn the heat on Keegan.

"Not knowing that Keegan was a psycho," Hardy said.

Keegan had, however, put up with it for a couple of years. Not only did he pay blackmail in money, but he gave them police protection when they needed it. Keegan's ambition was so great he would pay to keep things going.

"It was probably the death of Eleanor Payson and his son that sent him off the deep end," Mrs. Haven said.

"He saw a way to punish all of his enemies at once," Chambrun said. "He would murder Rogers and Bloomfield and frame Valerie Summers. He would be in charge of the case and it should be simple."

"Moving Mrs. Summers here made things too complicated for him," Hardy said.

"One thing I don't understand," I said, "is how he got Rogers to go to Val's apartment on Tenth Street and Willie Bloomfield to come here. He couldn't drag them by the hair of their heads or at the point of a gun. Rogers to Tenth Street maybe, but not Bloomfield here to the Beaumont."

"Money," Mike Maggio said. "They'd probably put the screws on him for more bread, and he told them he had a fabulously rich lady they could get to and milk. I wondered, you remember, how Willie could be wandering around the hotel without being spotted by one of my boys? He was with Lieutenant Keegan, the cop in charge of a murder. Willie just didn't look like Willie to them, I guess—in that kind of company.''

"How could Keegan persuade Willie to come here when his partner was already dead?" I asked.

"The story of the murder on Tenth Street had broken," Hardy said, "but it was twenty-four hours before the dead man was identified. Willie didn't know that Carl Rogers was in the morgue when he came here. The smell of money was strong enough to take him anywhere.''

"Once Keegan had started to roll himself down this mad path he couldn't turn himself off," Chambrun said.

"What's become of Paul Spector, the Tucson cowboy?" I asked.

Chambrun laughed. It was possible to laugh now. "He's trying to find a lawyer to sue the police department for keeping him from getting back to the penthouse. It's a good thing. If he'd been up there with you, he'd have tried to play the hero, and that would have been that.''

"How is Valerie?" Derek Newton asked, slumped in his wheelchair.

"It would be hyperbole to say she is 'fine,'" Mrs. Haven said. "She's been through an ordeal that most people couldn't take. I hope that Mark and I can help her forget and start living some kind of life.''

I smiled at her. "I'm sure as hell going to try, ma'am," I said.

Can you keep a secret?

You can keep this one plus 2 free novels.

FREE BOOKS/GIFT COUPON

Mail to: The Mystery Library™
3010 Walden Ave.
P.O. Box 1867
Buffalo, N.Y. 14269-1867

YES! Please send me 2 free books from the Mystery Library™ and my free surprise gift. Then send me 2 mystery books, first time in paperback, every month. Bill me only $3.50 per book. There is *no* extra charge for shipping and handling! There is no minimum number of books I must purchase. I can always return a shipment at your cost simply by dropping it in the mail, or cancel at any time. Even if I never buy another book from The Mystery Library™, the 2 free books and the surprise gift are mine to keep forever.

414 BPY BP90

Name _____ (PLEASE PRINT)

Address _____ Apt. No. _____

City _____ State _____ Zip _____

HOOKY GETS
THE WOODEN SPOON

 First Time in Paperback

LAURENCE MEYNELL

HOOKY HEFFERMAN WAS MUCH BETTER AT GETTING GIRLS IN TROUBLE THAN OUT OF IT.

His passion for the fair sex and English pubs aside, he had been known to solve a crime or two as a private investigator, profiting from the idiocies of this comic adventure called life.

Now he's been hired to find a rebellious, poor little rich girl who has taken up with some unsavory characters. Dad isn't comfortable swimming the murky waters of London's underground. Hooky, however, feels quite at home.

He's never minded helping out a pretty face—and Virginia Chanderley is that—but young and angry, she's also easy prey for a professional crook planning to steal a priceless painting. In fact, lovely Virginia has got herself into more trouble than even Hooky Hefferman—London P.I. and soldier of fortune—knows quite how to handle.

"Laurence Meynell had a gift for creating recognizable characters and ingenious plots."
                                                    —The Independent

THE CRUEL MOTHER

First Time in Paperback

A MEG HALLORAN MYSTERY

JANET LAPIERRE

**WERE THEY CAPTIVES BECAUSE OF SOME
MOUNTAIN MAN'S FANTASY? OR SOMETHING
COMPLETELY UNCONNECTED?**

Meg Halloran's romantic getaway with longtime love, policeman Vince
Gutierrez looks less appealing when Vince reluctantly introduces the
third member of their party, his spike-haired, foul-mouthed niece, Cass.

An accident with another car abruptly ends their plans. Then Meg and
Cass are inexplicably abducted, held in a secluded wilderness cabin in
Idaho's panhandle.

Meg desperately seeks answers—and a means of escape—unaware her
fate lies with strangers: a terminally-ill sixties radical who recently
confessed to murder; his wife, emerging from seclusion to reunite the
dying man with their young daughter; and a lawyer, calculating one of
the biggest scores of his circumspect career....

Available in August at your favorite retail outlet, or reserve your copy for July shipping by
sending your name, address, zip or postal code along with a check or money order for $3.50
plus 75¢ postage and handling ($1.00 in Canada) for each book ordered, payable to World-
wide Mystery, to:

In the U.S.	In Canada
Worldwide Mystery	Worldwide Mystery
3010 Walden Ave.	P.O. Box 609
P.O. Box 1325	Fort Erie, Ontario
Buffalo, NY 14269-1325	L2A 5X3

Please specify book title with your order.
Canadian residents add applicable federal and provincial taxes.

CRUEL

WORLDWIDE LIBRARY
™